NOT SO SILENT NIGHT

H.L DAY

BLURB

One grumpy patient. One unconventional nurse. Twenty-two reindeer later.
Things aren't great for Xander Cole. It's Christmas, he's fractured his pelvis on
a skiing trip he never wanted to go on, and his on/off boyfriend is most definitely
off. No wonder he's not exactly full of festive cheer.

Ferris Night isn't having much luck either. His plan to take a break from work
before starting a new job has been wrecked by a flooded flat. With nowhere to
stay, he grabs the opportunity for a job as a live-in nurse with both hands. After all,
how hard can it be?

Xander doesn't need a nurse. Especially one who's far too flirty, far too
attractive, far too into Christmas, and far too good at getting his own way. But
Ferris has never faced a challenge that couldn't be overcome with a bit of charm
and perseverance. It doesn't matter how attractive Xander might be. He's immune.
Maybe.

As banter and sparring between the two men turn into more, a nurse might not
be needed, but both men could be in for a fresh start to the new year.

*A low angst 63k romantic comedy, which features snarky banter, a slow burn
relationship, two men who can give as good as they get, an annoying ex, and a
Star Wars nativity scene.*

CHAPTER ONE

Xander

As I tumbled down the snowy slope. I wouldn't exactly say that my life flashed before my eyes, but I certainly reconsidered a few of my life choices. Chief among them was letting my on/off boyfriend, Harvey, talk me into going skiing in St. Moritz. To say I'd been dead set against it was a huge understatement. I'd wanted to go somewhere hot. Preferably somewhere with a long expanse of white, sandy beach, where the sea was so clear you could see the marine life swimming beneath the surface. Harvey… hadn't. And as usual, Harvey had gotten his way, mainly because no trip was worth the amount of sulking that Harvey was capable of. If there was a prize for petulance, Harvey would win the star prize, and manage to be runner-up all at the same time.

I blamed his upbringing. While Harvey might be a world-renowned photographer in his own right, I couldn't help but suspect that his yacht-owning parents, and the circles they mixed in—Hollywood royalty and all—hadn't exactly hampered his choice of career. It made life a lot easier when you could pick up the phone to Auntie Susan and suggest a couple of pictures of her holding her newly acquired Oscar. I was probably being unfair. Who was I to say that Harvey Walker wouldn't have been successful without the head start? After all, he didn't exactly lack talent. My own modeling headshots were testament to that.

So, skiing it was. It wasn't that I couldn't ski, but I lacked the natural ability of someone who'd learned it practically alongside walking, and had perfected their technique year after year. And we weren't alone on this trip. Harvey had brought his usual entourage along with him: his manager, his PA, and two people who I hadn't quite worked out what they did yet, but they always seemed to be there.

They were all natural skiers, while I was relegated to the beginner slopes. Me and a pair of eight-year-old German twins, who it could be argued were already a lot better than I was. It sucked to be dumped while the rest of the group wandered off laughing and joking. By day four, I'd had enough and had convinced myself that whatever they could do I could do, well, not better. I wasn't quite that delusional, but I should be able to hold my own. How hard could it be? It was just another slope, which was a bit steeper and a bit longer than the one I'd spent four days skiing down. Improvement came with challenge.

The result. This... uncontrolled... I suppose there was no other word for it, unless I wanted to use the word 'fall' down the ski slope. How fast could a human body travel and still survive? But this was snow, right? Snow was meant to be soft, and no slope could go on forever. It had to end, and I had to come to a stop eventually. And once I had, I'd laugh at my own stupidity of thinking I was ready for this. I'd pick myself up, I'd go back to the lodge and have a very stiff drink, maybe some god-awful cocktail that had about twelve different types of alcohol in it, and then I'd get on a plane and go somewhere I wanted to go. Harvey could follow or he could stay here. I wasn't sure I cared much at the moment, especially given that he'd spent most of the previous night flirting outrageously with the bartender who hadn't looked a day over eighteen.

The fence came rushing toward me at an impressive speed. Although, I supposed it was the other way around. The impact was sickening, the air squeezed from my lungs and leaving me struggling to pull in enough oxygen. At first, I was glad to be alive. But then the pain started, sharp enough to tell me that something wasn't right.

Someone in a bright Day-Glo green ski suit came to a perfectly executed stop right next to me, Harvey lifting his goggles away from his face to peer down at me. "Jesus, babe, are you alright? I thought you were never going to stop. You were going so fast I could barely keep up." His words said concern, but the expression on his face was more amusement. The last thing I needed while lying in an ungainly heap at the bottom of a mountain was someone finding it funny. It was Harvey's fault I was here, with here being St. Moritz *and* the ski slope. Surely, I was entitled to at least a small amount of guilt from him.

He bent over, the expression on his face rapidly changing to something that could only be described as horror. "Oh!"

"What?" I lifted my head to see what had provoked the strange reaction. There was a piece of fencepost sticking out of my upper thigh. The wound around it was bleeding profusely, the droplets of blood startlingly red against the white of the snow. There was quite a lot of it as well. That wasn't good. Retching sounds came from my left. Harvey didn't like blood. I couldn't say I was a huge fan of it myself, especially when it was my own. I was spared the inevitable sound of Harvey vomiting when I passed out.

·♥·♥·♥·♥·♥·

Hospital. I had that thought even before I opened my eyes. It was the smell, that unmistakable mixture of disinfectant and illness. Someone had removed my ski gear, and the area below my waist was swathed in bandages. I tried to shift position, the immediate stab of eyewatering pain telling me that staying still was a much better option. Everything hurt: my head, my arms, my legs, my torso. I'd picked a fight with a ski slope and I'd lost. Or maybe it was the fence rather than the ski slope. It probably didn't matter either way. A nurse appeared by the side of my bed, her greeting in German.

I shook my head. "English."

She smiled. "I understand. We will speak English."

Her English, while heavily accented, was nigh on perfect. It was certainly better than my German. I doubted she would have been impressed by me asking for a pint of beer, or inquiring if she could please point me toward the nearest train station. "What happened?"

"You fell on the ski slope, Mr. Cole. We have many patients come to us from St. Moritz. It is our best customer."

I didn't smile at her attempt at a joke. "I meant... what's wrong with me?"

She nodded. "You have badly fractured pelvis, and also a deep... how would you say... laceration, I think that is the right word, in your thigh that needed stitching. The fractured pelvis will heal on its own, but I'm afraid these things are somewhat slow. You will be off your feet for some time."

While it wasn't good news, it could have been worse.

"You also have a slight concussion, and multiple bruises and contusions."

I nodded. No wonder I felt like I'd been hit by a freight train. Poor Harvey must have been beside himself with worry. Once he'd stopped throwing up at the sight of blood, that was. Was that why he wasn't by my side? "Is Harvey here? Is he okay?"

The nurse looked puzzled for a moment. "Harvey." She gave the name some consideration, and then brightened. "Harvey is the photographer, yes?"

My nod this time was eager.

The nurse gestured toward the door. "He is outside. Would you like me to get him for you?"

"Please."

She left the room and I waited, minutes ticking by after her departure. Had she forgotten to tell him I was awake? Finally, the door opened and Harvey walked in with his phone pressed to his ear. "...I know, right. I could have told them that. I completely understand, but trust me, it's not an issue. I can be there by tomorrow. There's a flight out of here in a couple of hours and I can sleep on the plane. James is already packing my bags as we speak. I just need you to send a car to pick me up at the airport." There was a long pause. "Yeah... great. See you then."

Only once he'd finished the call did his gaze drop to me. "Babe, you look better."

Did I? It had been what, a couple of hours since the accident? I wasn't leaking blood anymore, so I supposed there was that. "You can be where tomorrow?"

Harvey's face became animated. "Do you remember how that prick, Jason Danford, got the contract for the new Chanel perfume campaign."

Remember it. Harvey hadn't stopped going on about it for at least a week. He'd accused Jason of everything from blackmail to sleeping with every member of the team involved in the decision-making process. I nodded, a little voice at the back of my head asking me why we were talking about this while I was laid in a hospital bed. But then I had asked the question.

"Well..." Harvey's smile could only be described as wolfish. "Guess who got caught doing coke off a hooker? Chanel dropped him so quickly that I bet he's got scorch marks on his ass. Of course, they've offered me the contract, which they would have done in the first place if they'd had any sense and then they could have avoided all this. They need me to fly straight to L.A, sign the contract, and then get started."

I was confused. It felt like I'd gone to sleep in one universe and woken up in another. And I wasn't entirely convinced that mild concussion had anything to do with it. "When did this happen?" I had visions of Harvey on the ski slope, stopping mid vomit to take the call. He'd probably used me as a seat. "What about me?"

Harvey's brow furrowed slightly, as if he couldn't quite understand the link between the two things. "They said you're going to be fine."

"I've got a fractured pelvis."

The furrow deepened slightly.

"I'm stuck in Switzerland."

Harvey nodded slowly. "Do you need money?"

Money? If I hadn't known it would hurt like hell, I might have laughed. "No, I don't need money! I have my own money. And money doesn't solve everything." I had to be careful throwing out statements like that. The concept was likely so alien to Harvey that I ran the risk of him spontaneously combusting on the spot.

Harvey ran a hand through his hair. "Is there anything you need before I go?"

"Like what?" I didn't even attempt to disguise the disappointment in my voice, but if Harvey noticed he didn't react to it. His phone started to ring again. He grimaced, leaning over to drop a quick kiss on my forehead before straightening and checking the screen. "I have to take this."

He was already back on the phone before he left the room. Thirty minutes had gone by before I realized that he hadn't just left the room to take the call. He wasn't coming back. He'd abandoned me in the middle of Switzerland with a fractured pelvis.

The nurse came back a few minutes later. She took one look at my face and asked what I needed. I told her more pain medication and a phone to call my brother, not necessarily in that order. She sorted out both in record time.

Miles was there by the middle of the next afternoon. He'd dropped everything to get on a plane straightaway, and I loved him for it. He arrived in the hospital straight from the airport, looking rumpled and tired, and carrying a small suitcase that he hadn't bothered to drop off anywhere in his rush to come to my aid.

I blamed that for the fact that when he walked into the room all I wanted to do was cry.

Seeing my expression, he abandoned his suitcase in the middle of the floor and almost threw himself into the plastic chair at the side of the bed. "Jesus, Xander. What's wrong? Are they not giving you enough pain medication? Let me talk to the nurse. I'll get them to up it."

I managed a smile as I shook my head. "Just happy to see you, that's all."

He quirked an eyebrow. We had a fairly typical sibling relationship. We needled each other. We wound each other up. We both knew that we loved the other, but hell would freeze over before we ever said it out loud. Therefore, I'd just broken the unspoken brother code by expressing happiness at his presence. "Or maybe it's a case of *too much* pain medication, hey?"

I *was* feeling pretty floaty, the last dose of whatever they were giving me—I hadn't actually asked—delivered about twenty minutes previously. "Probably. But I am glad you came."

Miles smiled. "Of course I came. I was hardly going pass up the opportunity of having you at my mercy. I can say absolutely anything I want to you and you've got no choice but to listen to it." He reached over to pat my arm, the action at odds with his words.

"I want to go home."

Miles tipped his head to one side. "Where's home?"

It was a fair question. The reality of modeling meant I spent a lot of time flitting between various countries. I had a house in London, another in LA, and I'd been thinking of buying one in Australia but hadn't gotten round to it yet. "London. Home, home."

Miles nodded. "I just need to get permission for you to fly and then we'll go. You'll be home in no time."

I lay back and closed my eyes. Miles would sort it. That's what big brothers were for. I'd thought it was what boyfriends were for, but apparently, I'd been mistaken about that. Perhaps I needed a boyfriend who thought my health came before his job. A person like that had to exist, surely?

CHAPTER TWO

Ferris

"I can't believe you're leaving me."

The accusatory statement had come from the open doorway I'd just passed. A few steps back had me meeting Mrs. Brown's decidedly frosty stare. Damn it. I should have kept on walking and pretended I hadn't heard her, but it was too late now.

Resigned to having to explain myself, I stepped into the room, returning the smiles and waves of several of the other patients on the ward. Mrs. Brown wasn't smiling; Mrs. Brown was scowling at me. The expression on Mrs. Brown's face wouldn't have been amiss if she'd returned from a quick trip to the toilet to find me taking a nap in her hospital bed. I came to a stop by the side of her bed. "I'm not leaving you. We're not breaking up. I'm just changing jobs. I'm moving to a new place and the commute would have taken far too long to keep working at this hospital."

She crossed her arms over her chest, her chin rising in a mutinous fashion. "You could at least try it. Young people these days give up on things far too easily."

For such a small lady, Mrs. Brown was surprisingly fierce. She was a recurring patient, her unwillingness to go into sheltered accommodation, along with her propensity for falls, was not a great combination. Therefore, we'd spent a lot of time together during my three years of working at the hospital. It was almost enough to make me feel guilty. Almost.

I gave her an apologetic smile. "Trust me, it wouldn't work."

Her mouth settled into a thin line. "Fine. Next time the ambulance comes, I'll just ask to be taken to a different hospital."

I let out a snort. "I don't think it works like that."

An obstinate look settled on Mrs. Brown's face. "I can kick up quite a fuss when I want to, you know."

I didn't doubt it for a minute. After a quick glance at the door to check my supervisor wasn't passing, I settled myself in the visitor's chair at the side of Mrs. Brown's bed. Mind, it was my last day anyway. What were they going to do, fire me? "Please don't do that. The ambulance crew are there to get you help as quickly as they can. That doesn't mean driving you across to the other side of London."

She let out a huff. "What about my grandson?"

I frowned. "What about him?"

A wicked smile settled on her face. "You've seen him. He's a good-looking boy, right?" I nodded, still not sure where she was going with this. She tutted. "You and him should get together. That way you can be my son-in-law. I've never been to a gay wedding."

She looked very pleased with herself at the idea. I stared at her. "Your grandson is straight."

She let out a sound halfway between disbelief and disgust. "So he says."

"He's married with two kids."

She shrugged. "You could give it a go."

I leaned forward conspiratorially. "So... you're suggesting that I not only seduce a straight man, but that I ignore the fact that he's happily married. Just so you and I can have tea together regularly."

She nodded eagerly, her eyes shining with mischievous amusement. "All's fair in love and war."

She was a character. I had to give her that. Her body might be failing her now that she was in her eighties, but her mind was still sharp. I was going to miss her. Unless... "I tell you what... how about I come round for tea anyway?"

She sat up straighter in bed. "Yes! You should do that."

Smiling, I rose to my feet. "I will."

"Promise?"

"I promise."

She lay back against the pillows. "And I can make sure that Brandon is there. You can..."

I shook my head. "No Brandon. I'm not gong to try and seduce your straight grandson. I may not be an angel, but I draw the line at that."

She pouted at me. "You should have a boyfriend."

I smiled. "I know, but I'm holding out for a special one. Call me Mr. Fussy but I'd like one that's not already married, particularly not to a woman."

That was Mrs. McGilling's cue to pipe up from the next bed. "There's a man who works in the butchers near me. I'm pretty sure he's gay. What about him?"

Mrs. Murs clicked her tongue from the other side of the room. "I know a gay hairdresser. At least I think he's gay. He'd be a better choice. He can do your hair."

"You can get free meat from the butcher."

And he might give me sausages from work as well.

"Brandon has an excellent life insurance policy."

"But he can't do hair, can he?"

"Maybe your new hospital will have a sexy doctor."

"You don't want a doctor. They might get paid well, but they work really long hours. You'll never see him."

"Butchers only work nine till five."

"So do hairdressers."

"The hairdressers near me stay open till late. I usually go there on a Tuesday evening when it's quiet."

"How about a fireman?"

"A bit too dangerous. You'll never be sure that he's going to come home. Plus, think about trying to get the smell of smoke out of his clothes."

I left them to it, none of them seeming to notice my departure as they continued to argue over who'd make the best boyfriend. It seemed to have slipped their minds that the boyfriend was meant to have been for me.

·♥·♥·♥·♥·♥·

As last days went, it had gone well. There'd been cake. Most of it eaten by me. Tears—none of them shed by me. Okay, maybe one or two had, but they really should have known better than to try and take the last piece of cake. I was laden down by gifts as I shouldered my way through the door to my flat. The first clue that something wasn't right was the water up to my shins as I entered the living room.

I stood and stared at the pot plant floating toward me. It seemed quite happy. Probably because I hadn't watered it for a while, and now it thought it was self-sufficient and had all the water it could possibly ever need. I waded through the lake in an effort to find its source because I might not be an expert, but even I knew that water didn't just teleport out of thin air. The bedroom revealed nothing, but the kitchen was a different matter entirely. There was a hole in the ceiling, with water pouring through it like a mini waterfall. Not good. My phone rang and I answered it without looking at the caller ID. "Hello."

"Ferris?"

"Yeah." It was my mum. It was like she could smell a disaster at five hundred feet.

"I can barely hear you. Is that water I can hear?"

"It is. I'm in the kitchen."

"Turn the tap off."

I looked down at the water that had risen another inch. "I wish it was that easy. My flat's flooded."

"How?"

I shrugged. "I don't know. I just got home. It's coming from the flat upstairs. I guess they had some sort of problem."

"How deep is it?"

"Deep enough."

"Well, you can't stay there, then."

I'd already come to that conclusion.

"Can you move into your new place?"

That would have been the perfect solution. I already had a new flat lined up closer to my new workplace. "Afraid not. It won't be ready for another couple of weeks."

"Oh!" There was a long pause. "What about Jonathan? Didn't he have a spare room?"

I waded back to the living room. "You think I should ask my ex, who I happen to have dumped, if I can stay in his spare room?"

"You could get back with him."

"You're seriously advocating rekindling a relationship just so I have a place to stay. Thanks, for that, Mum. I'd rather get with Brandon. I think he's got a caravan in Skegness. I can be his mistress until I bring him over to the dark side completely."

"Who's Brandon?"

I sighed. "Never mind."

"You can stay with us."

I grimaced. I'd known the offer was coming. "You don't have room."

"We can clear out the stuff in the spare room. It's only for a couple of weeks. We can squeeze it in the garage. Barry won't mind."

I bet he wouldn't. And therein lay the problem. Barry was my mum's boyfriend. He happened to be a good eight years younger than her, which I think had a lot to do with why she acted like the sun shone out of his backside. Unfortunately, Barry had a serious case of the wandering eye, and he wasn't too fussy about where it wandered to. He wasn't stupid enough to flirt with me while she was in the room, but had no such qualms about doing it when her back was turned. I was well aware that the best thing to do would be to tell her, but I just hadn't been able to bring myself to be the one to break her heart. I'd figured she'd find out on her own eventually, but it hadn't happened yet.

"Come round and we'll talk about it."

"Is Barry in?"

"No, he's gone out. Why?"

I ignored the question. "I'll find out what's going on and then I'll come round."

"See you soon, love."

We said our goodbyes and I hung up. I narrowed my eyes at the pot plant as it floated past again. "Don't get used to this. You'll be back to strict rations soon."

·♥·♥·♥·♥·♥·

I took a sip of the tea that my mum had made. "So yeah, apparently their water tank burst... directly into my flat. My landlord is understandably pissed, considering he still hasn't found a new tenant and he was hoping to be able to show people around. Which unless he can find someone who wants to practice their canoeing in the living room, he's going to be out of luck until it all gets cleaned up. And then of course he's going to need to redecorate first. All the carpets will be ruined."

My mum reached over to pat my hand. "What about your stuff?"

"Most of it is okay. The water didn't reach that high and I'd already started packing some of it up. I'll pack the rest and put it into storage."

The front door banged, Barry walking into the kitchen a minute later. He stood in the doorway smiling in a way that made me want to punch him in the face. "What's this?"

My mum got up and gave him a kiss on the cheek, and it was all I could do not to let my lip curl.

"Ferris's flat flooded. I said he could stay here. You don't mind, do you?"

Barry didn't hesitate. "Of course not. You're welcome to stay, Ferris. What's that Spanish saying... *mi casa et su casa.*"

My mum looked pleased. I wasn't. I was even less pleased when my mum disappeared out of the room to go to the toilet and left the two of us alone. This was exactly the scenario I usually went out of my way to avoid.

Barry crossed his arms over his chest. "There's always a bed for you here, Ferris."

Was I reading things into his words that weren't there? What if Barry didn't mean it as a double entendre at all, and I just had a dirty mind? Maybe if I came and stayed here, I'd realize he wasn't such a bad guy after all and I'd been misjudging him.

Barry's grin grew wider, his gaze sliding down the length of my body and lingering on my crotch. "I'll even warm it for you."

So much for that theory. Yeah, I wasn't staying here. I'd rather sleep in the street. Either I'd end up killing him or the whole thing would blow up into one huge, great family drama. I didn't have to be psychic to know that. I stood. "Tell Mum that I had a better offer, would you?"

CHAPTER THREE

Xander

December 1st

Still woozy from sleep, I tried to turn over in bed, the usual orchestra of pain flaring to life to ask me whether I thought it was worth it. The answer was simple —no, it wasn't. It was much better to simply lie there. I turned my head to the side so that I could see the illuminated figures on the clock on my nightstand. Four o'clock in the afternoon. By my calculation I'd been asleep for close to three hours. The side effects from the painkillers I'd been taking really were something else.

Every time I woke from one of my almost comatose naps, I resolved to stop taking them, convincing myself that the pain wasn't bad enough to put up with a head that felt like someone had replaced my brains with a wet sponge, and a tongue that always made me question whether I'd taken up sleepwalking to the beach and licking the sand. But the excruciating pain if I didn't take them inevitably had me changing my mind. It was like I was stuck in an endless cycle of regret.

My bedroom door was open, strains of conversation floating down the hallway. I could tell Miles was attempting to speak in a hushed voice so as not to wake me. Too late for that.

"… you must have someone available. Yes, I'm well aware Christmas is coming. I can read the calendar and it happens in December every year. At the same time as well."

Miles changed his tack, turning on the charm as he seemed to realize that his slightly abrasive tone wasn't going to be successful, and there were better methods of getting what he wanted. "I just need someone for a few weeks while I'm away, that's all. Maybe check your computer again. There might be someone you've overlooked. I'm not fussy about age or gender. Anyone will do, really, as long as they're qualified."

There was a long pause during which I pictured the expression on Miles's face as he waited. Patience wasn't his strong suit. Mine either. We had that in common. "Well, thanks for nothing. Have a bloody good Christmas."

Footsteps sounded in the hallway, getting closer, and Miles appeared in the doorway. He winced when he realized I was awake. "Sorry, Xander. I was trying to keep my voice down, but she was so goddamn snooty and superior that she made it impossible. Plus, that was the fourth agency I'd rung. The other three weren't helpful either." His voice softened. "How are you doing? Want me to bring you some more painkillers?"

"Not yet." My voice sounded rusty and cracked, like I'd left it out in the rain for too long. Yet another side effect of the damn pills. I blamed them for the fact that my thought processes were so slow that I was struggling to work out what possible reason Miles might have for ringing around agencies. Then it hit me—they were nursing agencies. And the nurse was meant to be for me. "Hang on. Didn't we agree that I don't need anyone? In fact, didn't I expressly tell you *not* to look for someone?"

Miles crossed his arms over his chest and pinned me with a familiar stubborn expression. It was the Cole family look that said I'd just spouted utter bullshit, and he wasn't having it. My mum had had the look—God rest her soul, and even Miles's kids had it. Either it was genetic, or we all learned it abnormally fast and adopted it as our own. Miles waved an arm over my bed. "Look at you. You've got a fractured pelvis, in case you've forgotten."

I glared at him, proud that despite the medication turning my reactions to sludge, I could still manage it. "I'm hardly likely to forget, am I?" I gestured at the crutches leaning against the wall, close enough that when I'd psyched myself up enough to attempt leaving the bed, I could just reach for them. "Those monsters are there to remind me."

My brother ran his hand through his hair, leaving it in a state of disarray. "I'll stay. I said I'll look after you and I will."

Despite the immediate bright flash of pain, I forced myself into a seated position. "No, you won't. You'll go and spend time with your kids."

"Xander..."

His tone said that he really wanted to do exactly that, but that he was trying to be the better man. "Don't Xander me. It's been weeks since the accident. I'm on the mend. Besides, it's only for a couple of weeks, right? You'll have outstayed your welcome by then anyway."

Miles pulled a face, but it wasn't aimed at me. It was the same face he always made whenever his ex-wife was brought into the equation. Miles and Clarissa had met eight years ago. Theirs had been a whirlwind romance of fun and passion, marriage following in record time. Unfortunately, their breakup had been in a similar vein, Clarissa's move to Spain meaning that Miles's access to the kids was far more limited than he'd like. Around Christmas was the only time where he got to spend a few weeks with them. There was no way I was going to let him give up time with the kids to stay at home and nurse me.

Miles sighed. "I can't—"

"You can't not see your kids for Christmas. They're far more important than me. I'll be fine."

Miles's stare was long and considering, as if he was running the past couple of weeks over in his head and recalling every single moment where I'd struggled. Because I had struggled. The skiing accident had turned me from a fit twenty-five-year-old into someone who found the smallest thing difficult. My pelvis would heal. It *was* healing. But the doctors had made it clear that injuries like that didn't like to be rushed.

Miles chewed on his lip. "I'll call Harvey."

"You will not!"

I hadn't told Miles that Harvey had been with me in St. Moritz, and that he had scarpered straight after the accident. He'd assumed I'd been there for work and I hadn't bothered to correct him. I didn't want to have to admit that I'd been weak enough to let him charm me into going somewhere I hadn't wanted to be. In retrospect, it had been an even worse decision than I'd initially thought. Given my current state, I should have listened to my gut. It was doubtful that I'd have managed to fracture my pelvis on a beach in Acapulco. The cocktails weren't that heavy.

I'd spent quite a bit of time since getting back from Switzerland thinking about my relationship with Harvey. Back when I was eighteen and on my first shoot, I'd been warned to be wary of the attention of photographers. It was a rule that I'd lived by for many years. An hour with Harvey, being showered by compliments, and that resolve had bitten the dust, the two of us getting on so well that our first date had turned into our first night together.

Our relationship had never been perfect. Far from it. We'd broken up more times than I could count, but we invariably ended up back together, the two of us orbiting each other like satellites that couldn't quite manage to drift apart. Except maybe that had just been me. Harvey had managed to drift away from Switzerland in my time of need quite easily. If it hadn't been for Miles, I would have probably still been stuck in St. Moritz. "Harvey is..." I shook my head wearily. "He's probably already in bed with someone else."

Miles stared at me intently, as if he was waiting for the punchline. "What do you mean?"

I sighed. "Our relationship was pretty casual. Harvey always made it clear that it was about fun and good times, not..." I gestured down at my sheet-covered body. "You could beg him, and he still wouldn't find time to come back and look after an invalid. It's not his sort of thing."

Miles's jaw tightened. "Why have you never mentioned how flaky he was before? I thought you two had a good thing going."

A pang hit me, a pang which reminded me that in spite of knowing what Harvey was like, what he'd always been like, I'd secretly held out hope of changing him. I'd hoped that one day he'd slow down, give up his jet-setting lifestyle and settle down with one person—me. I might travel as much as he did for work, but I'd never needed to, not the way he did. "Because... it didn't matter, until it did. I don't want him here." That wasn't strictly true. No doubt if he turned up at the door full of apologies for his behavior, I'd cave just as quickly as I always had. But I didn't want him to come just because Miles had made him feel guilty.

Miles nodded understandingly. "You could come with me?"

I shook my head. "The flight from Switzerland to London was bad enough. I'm not doing that again. I'll be fine. I promise, I'll take it easy. I won't do anything stupid."

I could tell the moment when Miles caved to the inevitable. I knew how desperate he was to see his kids. Christmas would be fine. Being alone was fine. It was certainly preferable to being stuck with some do-gooder of a nurse desperate to treat me like a geriatric just because one part of my body didn't work as well as it had before I'd plunged down a snowy mountain headfirst and used a fence to break my fall.

CHAPTER FOUR

Ferris

Apart from a Great Dane trying to walk its owner, the park was empty. It was probably meant to be the other way round, but it certainly didn't look that way—the poor man being dragged along at a frankly alarming pace. I considered helping him, but the day's events hadn't really left me feeling up to wrestling a Great Dane into submission, so I lowered myself onto a wooden bench by the duck pond to take stock instead.

I couldn't stay in my flat. Not unless I was going to invest in a good pair of waders, forsake electricity, and hang from the ceiling like a bat to sleep. I couldn't stay at my mum's when it had taken Barry all of two seconds to slip another come-on into conversation. There wasn't even a lock on the bathroom door, so I really didn't fancy attempting to shower without Barry 'accidentally' walking in on me.

I had friends I could stay with, but none of them had a spare room. Therefore, it would mean sleeping on their sofa, which never failed to be exceedingly awkward. I'd been there and done that. I couldn't afford a hotel or a Bed and Breakfast for two weeks, so it looked like I was out of choices. My dear departed grandfather always used to say that something would always come up, but it just went to show that he'd been nothing but an optimist. Sofa, it was then. Or a range of sofas. I'd move on to the next once I'd worn out my welcome. I frowned as my phone started to ring, the number not one I recognized. "Hello?"

"Ferris?"

"Yeah, who's this?"

"Phil."

The name sounded familiar. I thought hard and it eventually came to me. I worked with the wife of his cousin. We'd bumped into each other at a few social events over the years. "Phil! How are you?"

"I'm good. A little bird told me that you're not starting your new job for a few weeks."

I laughed. "Figured I'd earned a bit of time off."

"Ah!" He sounded disappointed. "So you wouldn't be interested in a private job, then? I told Miles it was a bit of a stretch, that even if you were interested, that him looking for someone prepared to be there twenty-four-seven was a big ask. He's desperate to find someone to look after his brother. Apparently, all the nursing agencies don't have anyone available."

I sat up straighter. "Wait! When you say twenty-four-seven, do you mean it's a live-in position?"

"I assume so."

"Starting from when?"

"Straightaway, I think."

A slow smile spread across my face, and I said a silent apology to my grandfather for doubting him. "In that case, I'm interested."

"Yeah?" Phil sounded surprised. "Great."

"How do I land this job?"

"Meet with Miles, I guess. Convince him that you're the right person for it, that his brother would be safe in your hands. I don't think he's up for hiring just anyone. How about I ring him and sort out a time and place, and then send you a message? Are you busy tomorrow? I think he's on a bit of a time crunch to get it sorted."

I levered myself off the bench with a spring in my step. "Sounds good to me. I'm free anytime, just tell me when and where and I'll be there."

I whistled as I made my way out of the park. I could put up with one night on a sofa, and then all I had to do was charm the brother and the job was mine. Easy.

·❤·❤·❤·❤·❤·

Phil's message had directed me to a coffee shop. I scanned its interior, immediately spotting a man at one of the tables who looked like he was waiting for someone. I studied him covertly as I made my way over to his table. If this was the right guy, he was far younger than I'd expected him to be. I'd assumed that someone looking for a live-in nurse needed them for an elderly relative, but unless there was a huge age gap between the two brothers, that seemed unlikely. He was good-looking too. I came to a stop by the side of the table, the man lifting his head with a jerk at my presence. "Miles?"

He nodded as he climbed to his feet, his once over brief but definitely there. I held out my hand and we shook. "I'm Ferris." I gestured to the counter. "I'll just grab a quick coffee."

I was back within a couple of minutes. I took the seat opposite Miles's and studied the slight furrow on his brow. It was all too easy to guess what had put it there. I'd heard it all before. "I might not look like a nurse, but I am one."

Miles gave a slightly sheepish shrug, one that said he was embarrassed to be so easy to read. I extracted my CV from the inner pocket of my leather jacket and slid it across the table for him to read. I'd included a copy of my nursing certificate as well. I sipped my coffee while Miles carefully perused the information. The expression on his face was decidedly apologetic when he lifted his head. "This all looks good. What did Phil tell you about the job?"

I leaned my elbows on the table. "Absolutely nothing besides you needing someone quickly."

Miles nodded thoughtfully. "I'm flying to Spain tomorrow to spend Christmas with my kids. I'll be gone for a few weeks. My brother, Xander... Xander Cole..." He paused as if he was leaving space for some sort of reaction. As I didn't know what reaction he was after, I couldn't help him out by providing it. Was I supposed to have heard of him? There was definitely something vaguely familiar about the name, but I didn't have any idea why. When I didn't say anything, Miles carried on. "He fractured his pelvis in a skiing accident a couple of weeks ago."

I winced. "Pelvic injuries can be nasty."

"Xander says he's fine to be left on his own, but I'm not so sure. He's still in a lot of pain, and he's not that mobile. I considered not going to Spain, but Xander won't hear of it. I just..." Miles pulled a face. "I don't want to leave him on his own, especially at Christmas."

"Understandable."

Miles sat back and crossed his arms over his chest. "I've got to ask whether you agreed to take this job because of who the patient is?"

I stared at him. "I don't know. I guess that depends on who he is?"

Miles's lips twitched into a smile. "You've never heard of him?"

I shook my head. "The name's familiar but I couldn't tell you why." I studied Miles for a moment, trying to work out whether he was the sort of man who appreciated someone being upfront. Deciding he was, I leaned forward. "Can I be honest?" I waited for Miles's nod before I continued. "My flat flooded yesterday. I jumped at the chance of this job because I have nowhere to live until my new flat is ready. Phil said you needed someone who could be available twenty-four-seven, and I assumed that came with a bed to sleep in. Getting this job would solve an awful lot of problems for me. That's the only reason I'm interested in it. So... I'm sorry if your brother is some sort of bigshot and I'm meant to have heard of him, but I don't know who he is."

Miles's smile grew wider. "My brother has a lot of people who throw themselves at him."

I blinked. "Does he? Why? Is he covered in Velcro?"

Miles looked amused. "He's a model." He picked up his phone and tapped a few keys, turning it around so that I could see the picture on the screen. I took it off him and examined it. It showed a man in a designer suit in a typical model pose, his head tilted to one side to show off the razor-sharp cheekbones, his green eyes issuing a come on to anyone who cared to glance at the photo. I couldn't even tell what he was advertising. I didn't care. I'd buy it. Hell, I'd get three. He was fucking gorgeous. I wasn't about to admit that, though. I peered at the screen closely. "Are you sure he's a model? Were they short-handed that day?"

Miles threw his head back and laughed. "I like you."

"So... do I get the job?" I tried not to sound too eager, but it was probably a wasted effort when I'd already told him why I wanted the job so much. I'd slept on Emma's sofa last night and I didn't know where she'd got it from, but I was sure that I still had imprints of the springs in my backside. I'd probably need to admit myself to the geriatric ward if I had too many more nights like that. Mind, it was still better than getting sleazed over by Barry while my mum floated around believing everything was hunky dory.

Miles let out a sigh. "I should probably warn you that ever since the accident Xander hasn't been the easiest person to get along with. And I'm saying that as his brother. He's not handling being immobile particularly well. He's not going to be an easy patient."

I smiled. "Did I tell you that difficult patients are my forte?"

Miles looked hopeful. "I don't think you did." He studied me for a few seconds. "So... you're up for the challenge?"

I looked him straight in the eye. Unlike his brother's, they were brown. "I live for a challenge." It wasn't a lie. I did. Life tended to grow boring without someone or something to challenge you.

Miles lifted his coffee cup and waited for me to lift mine before clinking them together. "I think... you might be exactly what my brother needs. I don't know where you came from, Ferris, but you could be the answer to my prayers. Xander will give you shit, though. And for that, I'm going to apologize in advance."

I narrowed my eyes. "He can try, but I'm far from a pushover. He'll need to learn that he's the patient and I'm the nurse."

"He won't be your usual patient."

"I'm not your usual nurse."

Miles laughed, his body language a lot more relaxed than when I'd first arrived. He looked like a man that had just had a heavy weight lifted from his shoulders. I was really looking forward to meeting that heavy weight. I hoped that Xander Cole in the flesh wouldn't be a disappointment.

By the time I left the coffee shop, we'd hammered out a mutually beneficial agreement and I had Xander's address scribbled on a piece of paper. I also had a new sense of optimism at being able to sleep somewhere without springs skewering me in the back. And as for Xander being more attractive than any man deserved to be, all I could say was that it was a good job my previous experience of dating a model had ended in disaster and made me swear off them. I had no intention of mixing business and pleasure.

CHAPTER FIVE

Xander

December 5th

Miles: *Problem solved. I'll call you when I land. You can thank me later.*

I only got a few seconds of staring at the text message before the doorbell rang. What problem? Solved how? Thank him for what? I stared balefully at my painkillers, which I hadn't gotten around to taking yet, cursing whoever it was for not having the courtesy to wait thirty minutes until I'd taken them and they'd kicked in. It took at least a minute to struggle to my feet, sweat breaking out on my brow as I jammed my crutches under my armpits. It took another minute to navigate my way out of the living room and into the hallway. In that time the doorbell had rung another five times. If it was carol singers, I was going to lose my shit. Was it a criminal offense to threaten children with a crutch? I guessed it probably was. I just wasn't sure I'd be able to hold back enough to care.

It wasn't carol singers. However, the sight that met me was equally as unpalatable, particularly considering the way the man on my doorstep was grinning at me. I was in pain, and sweaty from the physical effort it had taken to get to the door. Not to mention the fact that I hadn't been expecting visitors, so I was only dressed in an old bathrobe. I wasn't in the mood for whatever he was selling, and with a cocky grin like that, he had to be selling something. I was halfway to shutting the door when he stopped it with his foot. "Whoa! Xander, right?"

The fact he knew my name didn't mean anything, except that he'd taken his time to do his research. They probably taught that in Sales 101. Know your target. Smile and address them by name. Well, he was two for two at the moment. I shoved at the door, but it didn't budge. "I'm not interested."

His head tipped to one side, one eyebrow arching in a quizzical fashion. "Not interested in what?"

"Whatever you're selling, or whatever charity it is that you work for." There was nothing in his hands, but there was a rucksack on his shoulder, so whatever it was, was probably in there. I scanned his chest, searching for ID while definitely not noticing how toned it was through the shirt he wore. No ID. That figured. He probably thought he was above having to wear it. I made another attempt to close the door, but with his foot still wedged in it, it was a pointless exercise. Discomfort gave the rising irritation even sharper edges. "Don't make me call the police."

"The police!"

He looked completely taken aback. Obviously, the hard sell usually garnered a better result. Luckily, the fact that I'd been reading Miles's message meant I'd slipped my phone into the pocket of my bathrobe. I leaned more heavily on my right crutch, fishing it out and brandishing it in front of me. I paused, giving him a chance to retract his foot. When he didn't, I began to dial, deciding a running commentary was in order, just in case he was too stupid to realize what I was doing. "That's the first nine that I've just pressed. I'm now going for the second one, which I will follow with the—"

"Miles sent me."

I froze, lifting my head to stare at him.

"Your brother."

"I know who Miles is. I've known him for twenty-five years. I just don't know who the hell you are."

The man nodded. "We should probably start again. I'm Ferris."

I cleared the 9's from my phone screen in case my thumb inadvertently slipped and I dialed another one accidentally. I had enough to deal with without the police tracing a silent call. "Like the wheel?"

His grin slid back into place. "Like Ferris Bueller actually, if you must know. My mum was a huge fan. Not so much of a fan of me avoiding school though, when I tried to live up to my namesake. Although"—he waggled his eyebrows in a suggestive fashion—"I have been known to give a hell of a ride."

He was flirting with me. What kind of weirdo flirted with sweaty men in bathrobes who'd threatened to call the police on them? Was that what did it for him? Or was he just one of those people who did it as easily as breathing? That was probably it. I bet if I put a cabbage on the doorstep, he'd flirt with that as well.

I shook my head, trying to dislodge the thought of him flirting with vegetables. What he did or didn't flirt with was hardly the crucial part of the conversation. I needed to find out why he was bandying my brother's name about and claiming to be there on his say so. I narrowed my eyes at him, letting him know that the flirting didn't wash with me. "How do you know Miles?"

Ferris gave that easy grin again, giving every impression of being oblivious to my suspicion. "I don't. Not really. It's more that we have people in common. Do you know Phil?" He didn't wait for an answer, pressing on regardless, either not interested in the answer, or already knowing it. "Well, his cousin's wife's friend works at the same place I do, or should I say did, because I'm currently between jobs. I left there, which is the only reason I'm free for a few weeks before I start a new job. Lucky for you, I guess. So yeah, I heard from Phil, and here I am."

My head started to pound. If there'd been an actual answer to my question there, I couldn't manage to unpack it from the rest of the information. There'd been an awful lot of words there that had told me nothing at all. I glanced down. His foot was still in the door. I rested my head against the door jamb, contemplating if I closed my eyes whether he'd still be there when I opened them. Deciding it was worth a try, I closed them, counting to five very slowly before opening them again. I reared back, almost toppling off my crutches. He was not only still there, but he'd moved closer, peering right into my face with a curious expression on my face. "Are you alright?"

I shifted position, trying to combat the soreness from one of my crutches digging into me by transferring more weight to the opposite side. My body was starting to scream "What the fuck do you think you're doing?" at me. "Never been better." I wiped away the trickle of sweat that had decided to punctuate my words by dripping down my face.

"We probably shouldn't be having this conversation on the doorstep."

I stared at him. "Or at all."

If he'd registered my less than friendly response, he didn't react to it. "We should go inside so that you can sit down."

Any restraint I had disappeared. "I still don't know who the fuck you are! I'm not in the habit of inviting strange men into my house." I bit down on the urge to add, *unless we've hooked up on Grindr.* Besides, that was pre-Harvey days. Although, given Harvey's inability to even pick up the phone when I called him, or to respond to any of my text messages, I guessed those days would be returning. The thought made me less sad than I'd expected. There was a twisted sort of relief at no longer being caught up in Harvey's whirlwind life of parties and being seen in all the right places. I might be a model, but I'd never fit the stereotype. I was just as happy—happier sometimes—spending the night in front of the TV.

"Let's go inside."

It was a definite sign of how weak and nauseous I was that I gave in, letting him steer me toward the living room, the door slamming shut in our wake. The journey back to the sofa was slightly quicker, probably as a result of me wanting to dislodge the fingers that rested on my back, which I assumed were meant to be helpful.

I sank onto the sofa gratefully, dragging in lungful after lungful of air until the urge to revisit my breakfast had finally begun to ease. Lifting a hand, I gestured at the bag slung over his shoulder. "What's in the bag?"

He frowned. "The usual. Pajamas, toothbrush, toothpaste, clothes, the book I'm reading."

I struggled to a more upright position, trying for a little more authority than my current slumped position allowed, and speaking slowly and clearly. "Why are you here? You said Miles sent you. I'm struggling to think why he'd do that."

Ferris's brow furrowed. "I'm a nurse. I said that, didn't I?"

A nurse! I subjected him to a long, slow scrutiny, taking in everything from the tight jeans and the leather jacket he wore that accentuated his lean, muscled build, to the fact he was incredibly handsome. I'd worked with less good-looking models on shoots. "You look nothing like a nurse."

He gave me a beaming smile. "Thank you."

"It wasn't a compliment." Except it sort of was, wasn't it? I was struggling to picture him devoting his days to changing bedpans and taking blood pressure readings. Half of his patients were probably in love with him, even if his bedside manner was horrendous.

Everything clicked into place. Ferris was what Miles had been referring to in his message, the so-called answer to a problem. I was going to kill him the next time I saw him. That could be my inspiration for healing. I'd push past the point where I could hardly walk just to be able to commit fratricide. Something else suddenly occurred to me. "Why have you got pajamas?"

Brown eyes met mine, a smile hovering on Ferris's lips. "It seems rude to sleep naked in someone else's house. I'm guessing we'll be sharing a bathroom, but hey, if you're cool with bumping into me in the middle of the night when I'm naked, then I'll quite happily leave them in the bag. I've got to ask…" The grin grew wider, edged with mischief. "…will you be naked as well?"

He was still flirting. I decided to ignore it. "Even if you are a nurse, I don't need one."

"*If* I'm a nurse?" Ferris shook his head, as if he'd decided that that wasn't the argument he wanted to pursue. "And as for you not needing one, you looked like you were going to keel over at the door. If I'd been here, I could have answered it for you."

I let out a sigh. "If you'd been here, there would have been no need to answer it because there wouldn't have been anyone outside to ring the doorbell in the first place."

"Good point." He eased his bag off his shoulder and lowered it to the floor.

Panic raced through me. "You can't stay here."

"Miles said I could. Miles said it would be fine. That was the agreement."

Miles was living on borrowed time. He just didn't know it, yet. I retrieved my phone, hitting the button to call him with far more force than it needed. It rang and rang, voicemail finally kicking in. I hung up without leaving a message, glaring at my phone as if I blamed the device itself.

Ferris cleared his throat. "He's on a plane."

I transferred my glare from the phone to him. "I'm well aware of my own brother's movements. I don't need you to tell me."

Ferris shrugged. "Just saying. You seemed surprised when he didn't answer."

I sighed. "Life is full of surprises today." I made an effort to gather myself. "Look, Ferris." I added his name to try and build a sense of rapport between us. The best tactic was to get him on my side, lull him into a false sense of security, and then kick him out when he least expected it. After all, it wasn't like I could use brute force, so guile would have to do. "I don't need a nurse, and Miles knows that. Even if it was useful to have someone to... I don't know, do the washing up or something, I'm not a complete invalid, I don't need someone here twenty-four hours a day, so you living here would be ludicrous. It would be a complete waste of your time. So—"

"That was for my benefit, not yours. That was the deal we struck rather than him needing to pay me." Ferris elaborated when all I did was give him my best steely stare. "I was meant to be moving into a new place. New job. New place. I was going for the whole shebang. Only, there was a flood in my flat, the old one, not the new one. Apparently, the people upstairs fancied an indoor swimming pool. So now I've got to wait until my new flat is ready. I needed a place to stay. You needed a nurse. It was fate, with Phil playing fairy godmother." He screwed his face up. "God, he'd look terrible in a dress. Too stocky and too bearded, not to mention the chest hair."

"Fate!" I couldn't have put more distaste into the word if I'd tried. "Well, you'll have to find somewhere else. This is my house, not Miles's, so he had no right to give someone else permission to stay here."

"I see. I guess..." Ferris turned his gaze to the ceiling, pasting a deliberately faraway expression on his face. "I understand. Even though it's really close to Christmas, and the hotels are all booked up, it shouldn't be a problem. I'm sure I'll find some sort of place that I can afford on nursing wages, maybe a crack den or a brothel. And if not, there's always the streets. Snow isn't forecast for a couple of days. I can always bed down with the drunks and druggies. Sell my body for a warm blanket when it does snow. Yeah, that sounds fun. You keep your spare room. I don't need it."

I knew when I was being played. It was extremely doubtful Ferris didn't have someone he could stay with, but even so there was a tiny niggle of doubt. What if he did end up sleeping on the streets at Christmas? What kind of person did that make me? And Miles wasn't going to be happy that he'd said one thing and I'd said another. He'd probably give me the silent treatment. Mind, I was going to kill him anyway, so that shouldn't matter.

Ferris sighed, long and loud—a move straight out of a daytime soap opera. He reached down, pulling his bag onto his shoulder in the best parody of it suddenly having been filled with bricks that I'd ever seen. I almost wanted to applaud. He could probably mime being stuck in a glass box really well too. He ran a hand through his dark hair in a gesture that screamed of a weariness that hadn't been there ten seconds earlier.

"I'll get out of your way then. Apparently, there's a soup kitchen that if you queue up early enough, they don't always run out. I need to find a box as well, one that's big enough to sleep in." He pulled his leather jacket more tightly around him, as if he was already starting to feel the effects of the cold despite my central heating being on high. "Do you have any newspapers I can borrow? For the box."

I shook my head.

He took a step toward the door. "I'll let myself out. It'll be quicker. I've got a soup kitchen queue to make, remember." He paused, the silence hanging between us. "I'll go then. It was nice meeting you, Xander." He took another step. "Have a lovely Christmas all on your own, and don't even give me a second thought."

Ferris moved out of sight, but I could still hear him as he made the trip to the front door even slower than I had earlier. "Halfway to the door…" Long silence. "Reaching for the door handle…" More seconds went by. "Opening the door. I'll be on the other side of it very soon."

I doubted that. I was pretty sure he could still stretch it out for at least another five minutes. I didn't know whether it was the guilt trip that had done it, or the mention of being on my own. Possibly a combination of the two. I laid my head back against the sofa and gave in to the inevitable. "Ferris!"

"Yes?" He'd completed the journey back into the living room in 0.2 seconds, which made it about four minutes quicker than his exit.

Even though I'd made my decision, the words were still difficult to force out. "You can… stay."

"Yeah?" The grin was back. "You won't regret it. You'll barely notice I'm here."

I'd known him a grand total of ten minutes, and I already knew that wasn't true. What had I done? What had Miles done?

·▼·▼·♥·▼·▼·

Ferris

I made my way up the stairs and into the room that I'd finally gotten Xander to admit would be mine for the duration of my stay. I gave it a quick scan: bed, lamp, chest of drawers, wardrobe. It wasn't that big, but it would definitely do.

My first encounter with Xander Cole hadn't exactly gone according to plan for a number of reasons. Chief among them was the fact that Miles apparently hadn't been brave enough to tell his brother that I was coming, which might have been okay if he'd bothered to inform me of that fact, but he hadn't. He'd taken the coward's way out and left me to be confronted by a scowling man threatening to call the police on me, which had been... Well, if I was honest, it had been strangely arousing.

I'd been somewhat shocked by my immediate physical reaction to Xander. He'd been pale, sweaty, and decidedly grumpy, and he'd still done it for me. I'd never intended to flirt with him, but the fact that the more I flirted, the more outraged he'd seemed to become by it had made it far too tempting.

Finding him attractive was something of a problem. But I had control, right? I could flirt without anything else happening. After all, he was a model. Miles had said Xander had men throwing themselves at him, so it wasn't like he was going to look twice at me. I was just a nurse. I didn't mix in glamorous circles. I didn't have the phone number of any A-list Hollywood stars. I was just me. Therefore, I could flirt to my heart's content, just to annoy him, and it would be nothing more than an amusing bonus.

Dropping my bag off in the room, I went to explore the rest of the house, starting with the upstairs. The first room I came to was a large tastefully decorated bathroom. There were two more bedrooms, one looking a lot more lived in than the other, which made me think the emptier one had been where Miles had been staying prior to his visit to Spain, and the other must therefore belong to Xander.

Anyone viewing the house wouldn't have known Christmas was coming up in a few weeks, given that there wasn't even the merest hint of tinsel to be seen anywhere. It was a nice house, though, if a bit sterile. I extended my exploration to downstairs, the kitchen full of every gadget you could possibly think of. I added trying them all out to my list of things to do.

There was no noise from the living room where I'd last seen Xander. What was he up to? I tiptoed in there, hoping to catch him in a compromising position. I grinned as I found him asleep on the sofa, his arm dangling over the side. I took a moment to study him, making an immense effort to remind myself that I was here as a nurse and therefore needed to consider his physical state rather than the long eyelashes and the way his bathrobe was gaping open to reveal a pleasing amount of tanned skin.

I had to admit that medically speaking his condition was a concern. Miles had told me Xander was on the mend, which I assumed he'd gotten ad verbatim from his brother. But the man I'd met wasn't on the mend. If he'd been doing his physio regularly, then I would eat... my hat. At least I would if I had one. I'd never been a hat person. They didn't look right on me.

But, yeah, Xander Cole was clearly the perfect example of the nightmare patient, the one too stubborn to help himself. Well, he was lucky. He had me now, and I'd soon have him back to his catwalk strutting best. I just had to make sure I kept my focus firmly fixed on my reason for being here—his health, and I didn't let it stray anywhere else. It shouldn't be a problem. No doubt, once he was feeling better, I'd discover that he was an arrogant son of a bitch. That would kill any attraction stone dead.

With one last glance at the sleeping man, I went to take a shower. Operation Get Xander Back on his Feet would commence once he woke. It might be my biggest challenge to date, but I was definitely up for it. He might be stubborn, but he'd met his match in me.

CHAPTER SIX

Xander

After my grudging acceptance that Ferris could stay, he'd wasted no time in making himself at home, disappearing to find the spare room so fast that should I have had second thoughts, I wouldn't have gotten a chance to voice them, which was probably the idea. I finally got to take the painkillers and, like most days, I drifted off to sleep, settling for the sofa rather than tackling the arduous journey upstairs. I had after all already been on a trek to the far-flung shores of Front Door.

Sensing movement in the room, I struggled back to consciousness,

"Who stole Christmas?"

Everything came back to me, Ferris—like Bueller, not the wheel—had moved himself in. I kept my eyes resolutely closed, unwilling to confront my brand-new house guest quite yet.

"I know you're awake. You think I don't have my fair share of patients who pretend to be asleep when I check up on them?"

I still wasn't convinced he was actually a nurse. "They probably do it in the hope you'll stop talking."

"Probably. It doesn't work though. Just for future reference."

I opened my eyes, and just as quickly shut them again. Definitely not a nurse. A nurse wouldn't be standing in my living room in just a towel. A small towel. One that didn't cover much. There was making yourself at home, and then there was making yourself at home.

"I took a shower."

"Evidently."

"Sorry. I would have asked, but you were asleep, and I didn't want to wake you."

As he'd made no move to leave the room to, I don't know, put some clothes on, I gave up on being polite, opening my eyes and staring at him unabashedly. My thoughts about his physique earlier had been right. He wasn't overly muscular, but there wasn't an inch of fat on him. He also seemed perfectly comfortable at being almost naked in front of a man he'd only just met. There were definitely worse sights to wake up to.

"So, you didn't answer my question."

I dragged my gaze away from his flat stomach to meet his eyes instead. "What question?"

"Who stole Christmas? Did the Grinch pay you a visit before I got here?"

"I don't know what you mean."

He rolled his eyes. "It's December."

"I'm aware of that."

"Well, there's not a single sign of Christmas in this house, and trust me, I searched for it."

I opened my mouth with the intention of saying that his search better not have included my room, except I was fairly certain it had. I could already tell that boundaries weren't his thing. Therefore, saying something would be picking a fight I couldn't win. "I'm not really up to decorating." Although true, it was hardly the full story. Miles had offered and I'd turned him down flat, asking him why he thought sticking up a bit of glitter and tinsel would make me feel better.

"I can fix that."

There was a gleam in Ferris's eye that I really didn't like the look of. "I thought you were a nurse, not a Christmas elf."

He hooked his fingers in the edge of the towel, the weight of his hands dragging it down to a level where he was dangerously close to revealing whether the drapes matched the curtains. "Darling, I am nothing if not versatile."

Since the accident, my libido had been dead and buried. When your whole focus was on riding the continual waves of pain and getting through to the next dose of painkillers without going crazy, the last thing on your mind was sex. Therefore, it came as a surprise that Ferris's double entendre was as successful as it was, my cock responding accordingly to his deliberate insinuation that he was just as happy to fuck as he was to get fucked. Unless, of course, it had been a perfectly innocent statement and I was reading too much into it.

I tried to sit up, a bolt of pain reminding me that I'd no doubt slept long enough for it to be nearly time for my next dose of painkillers. At least it solved the problem of arousal, my dick deciding it wasn't back in the world of the living after all. Tears of frustration sprang to my eyes. I hated this, hated feeling like I'd skipped decades and gone straight to being a geriatric. But most of all, I hated the look of sympathy I could see in Ferris's eyes. If I wasn't mistaken, there was an element of guilt as well, as if I'd roused him from his flirting and given him a stark reminder of his reason for being here.

Sure enough, he straightened to his full height, looking serious for the first time since I'd met him. "Right. I'm going to go and get dressed, and then we can discuss all the medical stuff, like what medications you're taking, what your pain scale is currently, and how you've been doing with your exercises. Hopefully with me here, we can get you looking a hell of a lot better in a few days than you currently do, because I gotta tell you, Xander, you should be further along than this, which tells me that you've not been doing everything you were supposed to."

I didn't get a chance to argue, Ferris sweeping out of the room before I could. When he returned, he was dressed in jeans and a jumper, only his feet still bare. That wasn't a problem, not unless I had some sort of previously unrealized foot fetish. He was also carrying a medical kit. "Did you steal that?"

He stopped by the edge of the sofa, peering at me with his brow furrowed. "I'm a nurse."

"So you keep telling me."

"Do you think I'm some sort of weirdo that pretends to be, in order to gain access to men who can't fight me off?"

I stared at him. "I didn't, but now I do."

He pulled a blood pressure cuff out of the bag, glaring at me when I tried to resist his attempts to wrap it around my arm. "I just need some painkillers. They're in the kitchen. If you want to be helpful, you can get them for me."

"I will." He tightened the cuff, pumping it up until I felt like my arm was being squeezed by an extremely over-amorous python. "After."

I watched him as he studied the dial, grudgingly admitting that in all probability, he was a nurse. No one could fake that degree of fascination in a set of numbers.

"Your blood pressure is high."

I shrugged, not sure what he expected me to say in response to that. Maybe he expected an apology for a bodily function I had little control over. I resisted the temptation to tell him that him standing there in a towel probably hadn't helped. He leaned closer and I got a faint whiff of shower gel—my shower gel. Him smelling like me, or smelling how I should if I'd actually bothered to shower in the last two days, was strangely alluring.

"You need to relax more. It will help your blood pressure."

I snorted. "I spend half the day asleep. I'm not sure I can get much more relaxed without slipping into a coma."

"Then we'll look at your medication. See if we can wean you off some of it. It's a good thing I'm here."

I rubbed my arm as he released the blood pressure cuff. I preferred it when he was flirting. The professional side of him was just annoying, and precisely the reason I hadn't wanted a nurse. "Yeah, good job! I don't know how I would have managed without someone telling me that my blood pressure was high."

Ferris's hands dropped toward my crotch, and I batted them away. "Hey, what are you doing? We haven't even had dinner."

He gave me a long, hard stare. "Examining your pelvis. You know, the bit that has a healing fracture. I want to see how painful it is. It's possible that we might need a hospital check if things aren't progressing as they should."

Heat rushed to my cheeks. Of course, that's what he'd been doing. I was hardly a vision of loveliness in my bathrobe, certainly not to the point where someone wouldn't be able to resist copping a feel. "No underwear."

"Pardon."

He'd heard. I might have mumbled it, but it hadn't been that quiet, considering his proximity. "I said…" I raised my chin so that I was looking him square in the eye. "I'm not wearing any underwear."

His lips twitched. "Can you say that again, but a bit slower, and if you could make it a bit huskier that would be nice. Also, if you could do it without the glare."

"Do you sexually harass all your patients?"

Ferris raised an eyebrow. "No, they're not normally that lucky."

Arrogant son of a bitch. He might be good-looking, but he wasn't irresistible.

"Besides… and I think it's important that we clarify this, you're not my patient. I'm helping out that's all. We're"—he tipped his head to the side—"in a mutually beneficial relationship."

"We're not in a relationship. There is no relationship between us." Great! Now, I sounded far too defensive about what had basically been an off the cuff comment. It was only when I got the usual Ferris grin that I realized it was the first time in weeks that I'd spent more than five minutes thinking about something that didn't involve pain and how to stop it.

·♥·♥·♥·♥·♥·

"I can probably find you somewhere else to stay." I had no idea why the idea had only just occurred to me. It was the obvious solution. It wasn't just a choice between him staying here or being on the streets. There were other options that wouldn't involve him being under my roof twenty-four hours a day, grinning, flirting, and wanting to do medical stuff to me. We hadn't even discussed how long he was supposed to be there for. Miles wasn't due back for a couple of weeks and there was no way I wanted Ferris here for that long.

Ferris raised his head from the meal of Spaghetti Bolognese he'd cooked, stopping with the fork halfway to his mouth. "I couldn't possibly put you to that much trouble. Besides, I've unpacked now." He waggled his fingers in the direction of my plate, the plate I'd barely touched while I'd been contemplating how to bring this strange parody of domestic bliss to an end. "Now, eat your spaghetti like a good boy."

A good boy! The urge to throw my spaghetti at him was almost overwhelming. Somehow though, I managed to resist. "You only had a bag."

"It was bigger than it looked."

"It was hardly the bloody Tardis."

"Yeah, but you know, there's the folding and the… It's just better if I stay here. I don't want to put anyone else out."

Funny, how he was fine with putting me out. I'd obviously wronged someone in a past life, and it had come back to bite me in the ass. "Where's the rest of your stuff?"

He chewed and swallowed before answering. "At my mum's."

"Can't you stay there?"

A shadow crossed his face. "I could, but I don't know how many days I'd last before I killed her boyfriend. Surely, you don't dislike me enough to want me to go to prison for murder?"

I didn't dislike him at all. That was the problem. If anything, and despite our short acquaintance, I liked him too much. If I'd bumped into him in a club, I'd probably have made a beeline for him. In a club though, I wouldn't have been a pathetic mess doped up on painkillers and unable to walk even a few steps without breaking into a cold sweat. It might sound bigheaded but Xander Cole in his prime was a sight to behold. Xander Cole—recovering patient, not so much. "What's wrong with your mum's boyfriend?"

Ferris put his fork down, as if even the thought of him had spoiled his appetite. "Nothing, in her eyes. My mum thinks he's the most perfect man ever to have walked the Earth. She won't hear a bad word said against him."

"And in your eyes?"

He shook his head. "Doesn't matter."

I drummed my fingers on the table, trying to decide whether to let it drop. It was clear that whatever it was, he didn't want to talk about it. Unfortunately, that just made me even more intrigued. "What does he do?"

"He's just a slimeball. Let's just say he wouldn't be averse to having something going on with mother *and* son."

"Oh!"

"Yeah, oh."

I stared at the top of his head as he went back to eating. I had to admit that the food was definitely a step up from Miles's attempts to cook over the last few weeks. I'd forgotten what things tasted like when they weren't either boiled to fuck or charred beyond recognition. Miles seemed to have a pathological fear of food poisoning when it came to cooking. He gave everything the time it needed and then added another hour just to be on the safe side. "You can stay here."

Brown eyes met mine, amusement sparking in their depths. "You keep saying that, and then five minutes later, you try and wriggle out of it again. If you were more mobile, I'd be concerned about waking up to discover that you'd packed my bag."

"Lucky for you then, that you'd hear me crashing into things in the dark."

"That's me all over—lucky!"

There was more cynicism in his voice than I'd expected from someone who'd projected such a happy go lucky persona all day, but then he had just been telling me about his mother's slimeball of a boyfriend. Add that to the fact that he was temporarily homeless, and I guess I could see where he was coming from. The best course of action was to change the subject. "I should take a shower."

"You should."

"That bad, hey?"

All I got in response was a slight eyebrow raise.

I ran a hand over the growth on my face, trying to remember how long it had been since I'd last shaved. There hadn't seemed any point with only Miles to impress. The thought stopped me cold. If I was already thinking about impressing Ferris, I was fucked. "I should shave as well."

He paused from eating, sitting back and subjecting me to a prolonged scrutiny that made me want to take the statement back. Finally, he shrugged. "Up to you. I quite like the rough and ready look."

I hid a smile at the compliment. Harvey had never been a fan of the unshaved look, and he'd let me know that in no uncertain terms on more than one occasion.

"What's put that dark and stormy look on your face? Sorry, dark and stormier look, I mean."

I lifted my gaze to find Ferris staring at me quizzically. There was no way in hell I was ready to discuss the complexities of my relationship with Harvey with a virtual stranger. Pushing my empty plate away, I shuffled carefully back in the chair. Sitting was still painful. Not as painful as standing, and definitely not as painful as walking, but still painful. At least my wince stopped Ferris from inquiring further. He propped his hand on his chin and leaned forward. "I bet I already know the answer to this question, but I'm going to ask it anyway. Have you been doing your physio exercises?"

The fact that I dropped my gaze was evidently answer enough, Ferris unleashing a weary sigh. "Thought so. I've got to tell you that if I had a pound for every time I've had this same conversation, I could have given up nursing a long time ago and retired."

I felt pushed into defending myself. "Have you got any idea how painful those exercises are?"

"Do *you* have any idea how much they speed up healing?" He gestured over at my crutches leaned up against the kitchen wall. "You should be far more mobile by now. You could have gotten rid of those things and be using a cane. The saying, no pain no gain, could not be truer when it comes to injuries like yours. You've got to suffer in the short term to get the benefit in the long term." He crossed his arms over his chest, his jaw setting mutinously. "Tomorrow, we'll start intensive physio. The aim is to have you off those crutches by Christmas." He held up a finger just as I was about to interrupt and point out that his timeline seemed ridiculous. "That's my promise to you. You'll hate me. You'll want to kill me, but you'll thank me in the end."

I decided against telling him that I already hated him. Apparently, the dark soul of a demon lurked beneath the pretty exterior. I gave silent contemplation to gifting the house to him and running away. Except, I had to be able to walk first.

CHAPTER SEVEN

Xander

December 6th

I almost didn't recognize the man staring back at me in the mirror. Super nurse Ferris had set up a chair for me in the bathroom, and I'd ended up shaving after all. Combined with a shower and a decent night's sleep, I looked far more human than I had in ages. I'd also discarded the bathrobe in favor of sweatpants and a T-shirt. I wouldn't be winning any style awards, but it gave me renewed hope of turning some sort of corner.

The bathroom door flew open, narrowly avoiding knocking me off my crutches, Ferris standing there with a huge smile on his face. He let out a long, low whistle, his gaze raking me from head to toe. "Well, would you look at that. Who are you, and what did you do with the grumpy man who opened the door to me yesterday?" He came a step closer. "Did you murder him? Cause I've got to tell you, I quite liked him. He was all brooding and intense. I hope he comes to visit sometimes."

I gave him a look meant to reduce him to tears, but it just made his smile grow wider. I sighed. "I can feel his presence growing ever closer. He seems to react to your voice."

He laughed, the insult bouncing off him like water off a duck's back. "Come on, let's get you downstairs. I've made breakfast."

"Yeah?" The torturous trip down the stairs might just be worth it if there was something worthwhile waiting at the bottom. Going down the stairs was always worse than coming up, the concentration and coordination needed like running a marathon. Miles had always left me to it, but Ferris insisted on coaching me through each and every step, as if I hadn't been traversing them with crutches for weeks. By the time I'd reached the bottom, it felt like the new man I'd seen in the mirror had fallen down the stairs and was currently lying in a heap at the bottom of them.

I hobbled my way into the kitchen, stopping dead at the sight that met me on the kitchen table: two bowls, a box of cornflakes, and milk.

Ferris spread his arms wide. "Voila. Breakfast."

I felt like a man who'd been promised a ride in a Porsche, and then been bundled into the back of a Mini. Ferris grabbed my arm, taking my weight as I shed the crutches and maneuvered myself onto the chair.

"You look like I've just slapped you in the face with a wet fish."

"You knew what I thought you meant when you said you'd made breakfast. You did that deliberately." I couldn't stop myself from sounding like a sulky teenager. He eased himself into the chair opposite, adding insult to injury by offering the box of cereal to me. I snatched it from him, pouring it into the bowl with as much attitude as I could muster and adding milk.

Ferris watched me with an amused look on his face. "I'm guessing you would have preferred something else. To be honest, I wasn't sure what your dietary requirements were. I dated a model once, and he would just about run screaming if anything was put in front of him that contained sugar or fat. He seemed to take it as a personal affront, like I was fattening him up for Christmas or something. We didn't last long. I couldn't take any more restaurant visits where I ate a meal, and he just nibbled on a lettuce leaf." He pulled a face. "Actually, it was nothing to do with that. That was just one symptom of his extreme vanity." He poured the cornflakes into his bowl. "I resolved never to date another model after that. They're far too high maintenance."

There was a lot to unpack in what he'd said. First and foremost, it confirmed that he was gay, or at least bisexual. He might have been flirty, but I'd met flirty straight men before, even been burned once or twice when I'd pursued what I'd assumed was a sure thing, only to be shot down in flames. Secondly, Ferris had sworn off models, which meant the first part about him liking men didn't matter, given that I was one of those models he'd sworn off.

I wanted to tell him that I wasn't high maintenance, but it would sound too much like an invitation to date me, which I wasn't offering to a man I'd known less than twenty-four hours. Was I? It was probably for the best that he'd drawn a line in the sand. It meant we could flirt to our heart's content without either of us thinking it would ever come to anything.

"Will you go back to it?"

"Huh?"

"Modeling."

"I guess so. I mean, yes. The fence that stopped my fall down the mountain wasn't content with just fracturing my pelvis. It gave me a free gift of a large splinter of wood, which needed stitches. I'm assuming it will scar, so my underwear modeling days are probably over though."

Ferris started to choke, his face turning red. I leaned forward to thump him on the back. The coughing finally ceased enough for him to be able to speak. "You have underwear pictures?"

I shrugged. "A few."

Ferris turned his spoon round and round in his fingers, looking thoughtful. "And where would one... find these underwear pictures should they want to look for them?"

"You want to objectify my nearly naked body?"

He held the spoon up in the air, a ghost of a smile on his lips as he used the spoon to punctuate his point. "Now, hang on, I never said that it was me that wanted to look at them, did I? For all you know I've got friends who are... underwear connoisseurs."

"Have you?"

He couldn't hold his grin back any longer. "I don't think connoisseur is quite the right word for them, but they'd undoubtedly enjoy looking at you in your underwear."

A frisson of something passed between us, the look in Ferris's eyes completely at odds with the fact that he'd just stated he wasn't going anywhere near a model ever again. I jerked as the moment was ruined by my phone ringing, Ferris jumping up to get it for me. I wished he hadn't bothered when I saw the name on the screen. "Miles."

"Hey, little bro. I meant to call you yesterday, but the kids wanted to go out for something to eat, and then I figured you'd be completely zonked, and I didn't want to risk waking you. How are you doing today?"

"Well, I haven't magically healed in the last twenty-four hours if that's what you're asking. I didn't have to stop running laps around the garden to take your call."

Miles's sigh echoed over the phone line. "You're pissed at me. I'm guessing you didn't appreciate my surprise then. I know you said you didn't need anyone, but I felt bad. So, think of it as being more to assuage my own guilt, than for you."

"You could have at least warned me."

"I know." Miles at least had the good grace to sound guilty. "But it was really last minute, and it killed two birds with one stone. He was in a bit of a bind with nowhere to live, you needed some company, and you've got a spare room, so..." There was a long pause. "And I met him. He's hot, right? I didn't think you'd mind a bit of eye candy around the place."

"Is he?" I lifted my head to look at Ferris, who wasn't even trying to pretend he wasn't listening. Swap the cornflakes for popcorn and he'd really be enjoying the show.

"Isn't he?" My brother sounded confused. "I mean, I know I'm hardly an expert on good-looking men given that I'm straight, but I thought he was pretty attractive." He paused. "He is still there, right? Please tell me you didn't throw him out on his ear. I know you said you didn't want a nurse, but I was assured that he's the most un-nurse-like nurse you could ever imagine. Not to say he's not qualified, he is. I checked it out. I wouldn't just unleash anyone on you..." He trailed off. "But yeah, it makes me feel better to know that someone is there."

"Oh, well! If it makes *you* feel better. Who am I to argue?"

"Xander!"

There was a great deal of weariness in my brother's tone. He was probably five seconds away from offering to fly back, which I didn't want him to do, given I was the one who'd talked him into going in the first place.

"It's fine. And yes, he's still here." I found myself holding Ferris's gaze. "It will be fine. Enjoy your holiday and say hello to the kids for me. Apologize for the fact that Uncle Xander can't be there." We both ignored the fact that I wouldn't have been there anyway. Harvey usually talked me into attending some sort of swanky party in New York or L.A. "Just tell them that their uncle discovered that skiing is not for him."

"Will do. I'll call you soon, and Xander, I know what you're like, don't kill the nurse. I'm not going to help you hide the body when I get back."

"The nurse has a name."

"Yeah?" My brother sounded surprised, not I assumed at the fact that he had a name, but at me bothering to correct him after such a short acquaintance with the man.

We chatted amicably for the next few minutes, until the sounds of children's voices in the background forced Miles to end the call and pay attention to them instead. I hung up, avoiding looking at Ferris's grinning face for as long as I could. Finally, though, there was no escape, not when he was directly opposite and less than a meter away. "What?"

"You stuck up for me. That's so sweet."

"I told my brother you had a name. I didn't rescue you from bullies."

"Would you?"

"Would I what?"

"Rescue me from bullies?"

This conversation was taking a very strange turn. "Have you got any?"

Ferris took a while to consider the question. "My sister's husband is not a fan of anyone of the homosexual persuasion. He likes to mutter obscenities under his breath when he thinks no one is listening. Maybe you could rescue me from him. He's not a bully per se, but…"

I stared at him as he got up to start clearing away the breakfast dishes. "Sounds like you've got one hell of a family, you know what with your mum's boyfriend and your homophobic in-laws."

"Yeah!" He loaded the dishwasher, before turning around with a glint in his eye that I didn't much like the look of. I was proved right by the next words out of his mouth. "Physio time!"

Cold dread settled in my gut.

·♥·♥·♥·♥·♥·

"I hate you!"

Ferris gave me a sweet smile. "I know. You're still going to do ten more, though. Just imagine that every time you lift your knee, you're kneeing me in the crotch. That might help."

It did help. Slightly. It still fucking hurt though, and all I was doing was sitting on a chair and taking it in turns to lift each knee. This was the first exercise and I was already a sweaty mess, desperate to take more painkillers despite having already taken some.

"What hurts today will help tomorrow."

I lifted my left knee once more. "Who the fuck said that? Whoever it was, I'd like to murder them slowly, so slowly that they'll beg me for mercy."

"I said it, but it's true, trust me."

"Figures. I'm already murdering you anyway, so at least it keeps the body count down."

"Five more. How are you going to murder me?"

"I told you, slowly."

"Yeah, but how? The method says a lot about the person doing the murder. Like the fact that you want to do it slowly means that you want to savor it. I'm guessing you're not going to poison me because that would be *too* slow, unless you can get your hands on some fast-acting poison. So that leaves us with how up, close, and personal you want to get. For example, strangulation often has a sexual element to it apparently, because you can't do it without getting really close. Do you want to strangle me?"

"You're so weird."

"I just find it fascinating, that's all."

I was beginning to wonder just who I'd let into my house.

"Lie on the floor."

I stared at him. He put his hands on his hips and met my stare, inclining his head toward the floor, as if my reason for not doing as he'd asked was because I'd forgotten where it was. "Can't we just stick with the one exercise today? You know, build up to it more gradually."

He let out a snort. "You should have been doing these exercises for weeks already, so no, we can't just build up to it. We need to get you to where you should be."

I looked down at the floor, but made no move to do as he'd asked.

Ferris sighed. "Three exercises, and you get a cooked breakfast tomorrow."

Bribery. Now we were talking. "What would this cooked breakfast consist of?"

"Lie on the floor and I'll tell you. Don't, and it'll be cornflakes again."

Oh, he was good. I had to give him that. "I can make my own breakfast."

"Not if I hide your crutches, you can't."

"That's mean."

He crossed his arms over his chest. "It's necessary. Don't make the mistake of thinking I'm above playing dirty tricks to get what I want, not when it's for the *patient's* benefit."

I knew when I was beaten. The process of getting to the floor was an exercise all in itself, Ferris having no choice but to help me, his hands, although professional, straying to places that I had to admit weren't unpleasant. How I was going to get up again, I had no idea. I pictured a Christmas spent on the floor, Ferris dropping bits of food into my mouth when he remembered I was there. He'd invite people round and they'd use my body as a table, Ferris waving a dismissive hand when they bothered to ask who I was.

"So, what do you want in your breakfast?"

I was grateful for his question stopping my lurid fantasies in their tracks. He crouched next to me, and I turned my head so I could look him in the eye. "Everything."

His face screwed up. "What kind of model are you?"

"One blessed with a very fast metabolism, who"—I reached out to tap the floor — "touch wood, will hopefully stay like that for the foreseeable future."

It was all I could do not to squirm as he subjected me to a protracted scrutiny, one which seemed to penetrate my clothes to what lay beneath. Heat flooded my cheeks and a certain part of my anatomy that would be only too obvious if it got any bigger, swelled in appreciation of Ferris's interest. "Okay. What exercise am I doing?"

His gaze trailed up my body until it met mine. "All of a sudden you're eager to do them?"

"Anything that gets me to the point where I can stand up again."

He joined me on the floor, modeling the exercise he wanted me to do, which was basically the same as I'd done in the chair and consisted of me lifting my knees to my chest, only in a supine position, it was much harder.

"You're doing well." Ferris's attempt to soothe really didn't help.

"Fuck off. Don't patronize me."

The snort of laughter didn't help either. At least my dick had started to behave again, the pain traveling along my synapses killing any thought of arousal stone dead. When I'd completed that exercise to Ferris's satisfaction, there was another one waiting. Only then did Ferris help me up off the floor, bearing most of my weight as he maneuvered me across to the sofa. I blamed my limbs being like jelly for forgetting to unwrap my arms as he lowered me. It left him with little choice but to follow me down. The result—him sprawled on top of me.

"Erm… Xander. Nice as this is, you need to let me go. I'm going to end up hurting you."

I wanted to ask him if it was really nice, or whether that was just another of his glib comments that I was beginning to know so well. I bit my tongue, giving myself another few seconds to enjoy the feel of his hard body against mine before releasing him from my octopus grip.

Ferris straightened, seemingly having nothing to say for once.

"Can I have a drink?"

He seized on the excuse with an eagerness akin to a starving man being offered a sandwich, almost running into the kitchen, and not returning for far longer than it took to pour the glass of lemonade that he eventually handed over.

Chapter Eight

Ferris

December 7th

I was seriously fucked. The more time I spent with Xander, the more it became an inescapable fact. I enjoyed spending time with him. I enjoyed winding him up. But most of all I'd enjoyed that brief moment of madness where he'd pulled me on top of him the previous day and hadn't seemed to want to let go. And I hadn't wanted him to. It had felt good to be pressed against him. More than good. It had made me forget that he was injured, leaving me about two seconds away from throwing caution to the wind and exploring how much of his actions might have something to do with a building mutual attraction. And if the answer was none, at least I'd have known. In the end, I'd had to run away to the kitchen and give myself a good talking to, spending far more time in there than getting Xander a drink warranted.

"Ferris?"

The call had come from the living room while I was in the kitchen. For a man who had insisted that he didn't need any help, Xander seemed to have overcome his barriers extremely quickly to demand that I was at his beck and call. "What?"

"What are you doing?"

"None of your business."

"That's not very nice."

"I'm not a nice man."

"Do you tell all your patients that?"

I tamped down on the urge to smile, not wanting him to hear it in my voice. "Only the annoying ones."

"Come in here."

"No."

"What if I'm having some sort of medical emergency?"

I rolled my eyes, even though it was wasted when he couldn't see me. "Call an ambulance."

"I'm calling you."

"I can't hear you."

"Why are you answering then?"

I stayed silent.

"Come here."

"You come here."

There was some pronounced mumbling, the words too indistinct for me to be able to tell what he was saying. Eventually, Xander appeared in the doorway on his crutches. His brow furrowed as he took in the empty table in front of me. "You're not doing anything."

I raised an eyebrow. "I never said I was."

He maneuvered himself over to the kitchen table and sank into the chair, resting his chin on his hands and staring at me. I stared back, refusing to notice how pretty his eyes were and how the faint stubble with him not having shaved that day only served to accentuate his features. There was more color in his cheeks than there had been when I arrived. By helping him to heal, I was in many ways making life more difficult for myself. He would only get more attractive. Xander narrowed his eyes at me. "Your nursing skills leave a lot to be desired."

I smiled sweetly at him. "I thought you said you didn't need a nurse. Therefore, I was going for the more hands-off approach." *And I really need to keep my hands off you.*

"You made me walk all the way from the living room."

I laughed. "'All the way from the living room.' Let me ring the Guinness Book of World Records. They're definitely going to want to know about a massive achievement like that. Today, the living room, tomorrow, Kilimanjaro."

He shook his head. "Surprised you're not expecting me to climb Mount Everest."

"That's next week." I mirrored his position so that my chin was resting on my hands too. "What did you want, Xander?"

He met my gaze without blinking. "I thought we could do my exercises early today."

I didn't even try and hide my surprise. "You want to do them early? You! The person who has spent weeks avoiding them, who lied to his brother claiming he was doing them when really he wasn't even attempting them."

A look of indignation settled on Xander's face. "That's libel."

I snorted. "Libel is written. I think the word you're looking for is slander. And…" I gave a dramatic pause. "It's only slander if it's not true. Did you or did you not allow your brother to believe you'd been doing your physio?"

Xander pulled a face. "What is this, a court of law?"

I waited him out.

He caved first. "I may have done… once or twice."

I sat back in my seat. "I rest my case. No further questions, your honor."

Xander heaved out a sigh. "Are you going to sentence me too?"

"I might. I'd have to think of a good punishment. I can hardly sentence you to hard labor. You wouldn't manage it without complaining."

"I have a fractured pelvis."

I leaned forward again. "I'm aware of that. That's why I'm here. If you hadn't fractured it, I'd be…" Where would I be? Fending off Barry? Sofa-surfing. I'd never expected to feel gratitude to a ski slope, but I did. I might be fighting a growing attraction to Xander, but I was still glad to have met him.

"You'd be where?"

I shrugged. "I don't know. Somewhere else." I got up, turning on the tap and filling a glass with water.

"I want a bell."

I frowned at the change of subject, pausing with the glass halfway to my mouth. "What sort of bell?"

Xander's smile was full of wicked intent. "The sort that I can ring when I need assistance." He lifted his hand and mimed the action.

I spun round to face him, my glare not needing to be faked. "Not a chance in hell. I thought you wanted to resume your modeling career. How are you going to do that once I insert a bell somewhere the sun doesn't shine?"

Xander quirked an eyebrow. "You have a really strange idea about the sort of photos I do, if you think that having a bell there would have any impact whatsoever. I think you're confusing modeling with porn."

I took a sip of water at the wrong time, nearly choking on it. I didn't need to be thinking about Xander having sex, whether there was a camera there or not. The thought was just too…

"Are you alright?"

I took a larger swallow of water to wash down the water that had got stuck. "Me? Why wouldn't I be?"

Xander's stare was far too assessing. "You look a little flushed."

I put the glass down and clapped my hands together. "So… exercises then. Let's do it."

I didn't wait for Xander to agree, needing the few minutes that it took him to get himself from the kitchen and back to the living room to calm my wayward thoughts.

Xander propped his crutches against the living room wall and lowered himself to the floor without having to be asked.

I went to stand by him as he laid on his back. "So why are you so keen today? I don't think we ever established that."

He stared up at me. "I just want to get them over and done with."

I nodded. "Ah, I see." I knelt next to him, my brain warring over whether I was eager to touch him or reluctant. Could you be both?

Xander tilted his head to the side. "I've never done porn by the way, if that's what you were wondering? It was just a joke."

I lay my hands on the area just above his waist, changing his orientation slightly so that there was less strain on his pelvis. "Maybe you should. You might be good at it."

A furrow appeared on Xander's brow. "Might?"

I laughed. "Oh, I'm sorry. I didn't mean to question your sexual aptitude. I'm sure you'd be fantastic if you put your mind to it."

Xander took a deep breath in preparation for the first exercise. "I would. I'd need a partner, though."

I encouraged him to lift his left thigh before I could do something stupid like volunteer as tribute.

· ♥ · ♥ · ♥ · ♥ · ♥ ·

Once Xander had taken his painkillers and disappeared upstairs for his usual drug-induced afternoon siesta, I sat and watched TV. The reliance on painkillers definitely needed to be tackled. They weren't doing Xander any good. In order for his health to keep improving, he needed to stay mobile, and being asleep for half of the day didn't exactly help with that target.

But… I'd decided that it was better to tackle one thing at a time, and the priority had been the exercises. Now that they were starting to take effect and I no longer had to bribe Xander to get him to do them, it was time to start weaning him off the painkillers. By the time his brother returned from his trip, Xander would be a new man, ready to assume his old life. The thought left an uncomfortable feeling in my gut.

Creaking came from above and I tipped my head back to stare at the ceiling, above which was Xander's bedroom. The far from model patient—I smiled at the accidental pun—was up. Sure enough, the sound of his crutches coming down the stairs followed. I'd helped him on the first day, but given how much he'd glared at me, I'd left him to it ever since.

He arrived in the living room a few minutes later, his hair sleep-tousled and his T-shirt rumpled. Anyone not spotting the crutches might have thought he'd just been fucked, the thought making my groin throb uncomfortably. I pulled a cushion over my crotch as Xander deposited himself on the other side of the sofa.

"Good sleep?" He threw a dirty look my way. "That good, hey?"

"I feel like shit."

"That's because…" I paused. This probably wasn't the best time. *Oh, fuck it!* "The painkillers aren't doing you any good."

Xander ran a hand through his hair. Instead of smoothing it down, it had the opposite effect, bits sticking up all over the place. "They stop me being in pain."

I twisted slightly so that I faced him. "The exercises will stop you being in pain. From tomorrow, we cut down on the drugs."

Xander leaned his head back against the sofa and closed his eyes, his T-shirt riding up to display a generous amount of toned abs. "We?"

I tore my gaze away before he opened his eyes and caught me ogling him. "Alright, *you…* with my help."

Xander let out a sigh. "Can't wait."

With his eyes still closed, he didn't see my smile. It was probably just as well. It would only have pissed him off. "Is this house yours?"

He opened one eye, turning his head so he could see me. "Yes. Why?"

I shook my head. "No reason. I was just thinking, that's all… you own your own house and I don't even have somewhere to stay."

Xander opened his other eye and I found myself the recipient of a very intense stare. "It's not a competition."

"Good job. I'd lose."

He sat up straighter, suddenly looking far more alert. "Modeling just happens to pay well, but all I do is stand around looking pretty. You save lives. It's just that society is fucked up and I get paid more for what I do than you."

He had a point, but unfortunately it served as another reminder that whether I thought he was the hottest person on the planet or not, we weren't compatible.

CHAPTER NINE

December 12th

Xander

Ferris was up to something. I'd learnt to recognize the slight smirk he wore when he thought he'd gotten one over on me, whether it was down to something as simple as what we were going to eat, or how many repetitions I did for my exercises. Which incidentally was always far more than I wanted to do. I had to admit though, that I was starting to feel better.

I was on the brink of asking him what was going on when the doorbell rang. From the way he sprang up to answer it, it was obvious he'd been expecting it. Dread settled in my gut as I listened to the low murmur of a conversation not loud enough to hear. The discussion—whatever it was about—was short-lived, Ferris reappearing soon after. He lounged in the doorway with his thumbs hooked in the waistband of his jeans, wearing that same smirk. "I've got a surprise for you."

I met his gaze head on. "I don't like surprises." That wasn't quite true. I didn't usually mind them, but surprises from him were a different matter entirely. I suspected they'd hold an unpredictability I just wasn't prepared for.

"Do you want to see it?"

It was like he just zoned out anything he didn't want to hear. And what was 'it?' I didn't like the sound of 'it' one little bit. "If I said no, would it make any difference whatsoever?"

He pondered the question for a moment before shaking his head.

"So why are you asking?"

"Good point."

He spun on his heel and disappeared into the hallway. He was only gone a minute and then he was back, my mouth falling open at what he was pushing in front of him.

I blinked a few times, but it didn't make any difference. I could still see the same thing. "What the fuck is that?"

His smirk grew more pronounced. "*This...* as you very well know, Mr. Cole, is a wheelchair. It's on loan from a friend, so don't get too excited. But... for one day only, think of it as your chariot, your key to rejoining the outside world. We're going to use this to go out. You're going to get to see something other than these four walls. You're welcome."

"I am *not*"—I spoke slowly so that Ferris could have no doubt what I was saying—"going out in a wheelchair."

His smile dimmed slightly. "Why not?"

"Why not?" My voice was pitched higher than usual, and I made an effort to drop it to a more normal tone. "Because..." I waved a hand at the bright red wheelchair. It just had to be bright red, didn't it? "I'm twenty-five."

Ferris crossed his arms over his chest. "What's your age got to do with it? You do realize that there are people of all ages who have no choice but to spend their whole lives in a wheelchair. Are you really going to kick up a fuss about spending one day in one?"

He had me there. I couldn't pursue that argument without making myself look like a total dick. Therefore, I tried another tack. "It's cold outside."

His lips quirked. "Says the man who went skiing. Did you stand at the top of the slope and ask them if they could please warm up the snow for you? I tell you what, if it gets too much for you, we can throw a blanket over your knees."

I gave him a particularly venomous look, his smile only growing wider in response. I liked it when Ferris smiled. I liked it far too much. He'd been cooped up in the house for days with me, only leaving to go shopping. Was that why he was so keen to go out? Would it kill me to go along with his plans just to make him happy?

Although, that begged the question whether he was just being polite by inviting me along. "You can go out, you know. I am capable of managing a day on my own. I did it just fine before you got here. You can go and see your friends, or do whatever it is you usually do."

Ferris tipped his head to one side and stared at me. "I don't want to go out on my own. I want to spend the day with you. And yes, I'll admit that lovely as this house is, it would be nice to spend some time outside it. But"—he lowered his gaze to the wheelchair—"If your macho ass can't handle me pushing you around, then I completely understand. We can stay here and... I don't know, put your socks in order from darkest to lightest, or"—he snapped his fingers in a way that said he'd had a really good idea—"you've got a bookcase upstairs. We can take them all off the shelf and put them all back on again in alphabetical order like we're in a library. Or—"

"I don't have a macho ass." I regretted the words as soon as they were out of my mouth, Ferris's gaze automatically dropping to that area.

"I can't tell. Turn around and let me have a proper look."

"Fuck off."

"Spoilsport."

"Pervert."

He laughed.

I eyed the wheelchair and sighed. I really didn't want to get in it. I'd had every intention of not getting in it, but he'd just had to go and say that he wanted to spend the day with me, hadn't he? How was I supposed to turn a plea like that down?

"Where are you suggesting we go?"

"It's a surprise."

Of course it was. "Fine. Whatever! I guess a few hours out won't do any harm."

·❤·❤·❤·❤·❤·

"The Natural History Museum!"

Ferris brought the wheelchair to a stop just short of the wheelchair accessible entrance, coming around the wheelchair to stand in front of me. "Got a problem with that?"

I shrugged. "I don't know. I just… it wasn't what I thought you had in mind."

He grasped hold of the arms of the wheelchair and leaned over me. It would only take lifting myself up slightly to be able to kiss him. Now, where had that thought come from? There wasn't going to be any kissing going on.

Ferris smiled, but it was distinctly wolfish. "Actually, I had the aquarium in mind, but I thought the temptation of feeding you to the sharks might be just that bit too strong. At least here, none of the animals are alive."

"Oh, really?" I arched an eyebrow. "I can foresee one very big problem with that scenario. Where were you planning to stay once you'd fed me to the sharks?"

Ferris slid his hand into his pocket and pulled out my keys, shaking them in front of my face so that they jangled. "I've got your keys."

I made a grab for them, but he was faster, pulling them out of reach before I could get to them. "Give me my keys."

"Nope." He rounded the wheelchair again and pushed me through the entrance. "Have you been here before?"

"Oh, every week. I just can't keep away from the place. It's all I think about when I'm on a beach in Miami."

Ferris flicked my ear. "Are you going to be like this all day?"

"Would you expect anything less from me?"

He chuckled. "No. Hence the consideration of feeding you to the sharks. A straight answer once in a while might be nice, though."

I leaned my head back against the headrest. Given my reluctance to get in the wheelchair in the first place, it had come as quite the surprise that I actually enjoyed having Ferris push me around. Maybe walking was overrated? I gave thought to his question. "I haven't been here since I was a kid. You?"

"Well, some of us don't get to swan off to Miami. We have to make do with things that are on our doorstep. So, it's only been a couple of years for me. It's my favorite museum in London."

I felt bad on two counts. Firstly, that I'd probably come across as an overprivileged dick by casually dropping Miami into conversation, and secondly because I was being disparaging about something Ferris actually enjoyed. "Sorry."

The wheelchair came to such an abrupt halt that I almost tipped out of it. "What was that?"

"You heard."

"I don't think I did."

"You should get your ears tested then."

"There's nothing wrong with my ears. I just couldn't believe that such a word would ever come out of your mouth." He pushed me into motion again. "We've come such a long way, Xander. Do you remember when you wanted to call the police on me simply for standing on your doorstep? Now, I get apologies. It's enough to make me go all warm and gooey inside. It really is."

I grimaced. We'd never actually addressed that first meeting. "I thought you were a salesman, a very pushy salesman who refused to take no for an answer." I had my brother to blame for that. If he'd bothered to mention hiring Ferris in any way other than a cryptic text message sent mere seconds before his arrival, then the whole thing could have been avoided. "And… I was in a lot of pain."

"And why was that?"

I rolled my eyes, even though Ferris was behind me and had no way of seeing it. "Because…"

"Yes?"

I sighed. I guessed I could give him this one victory. It could be my penance for dissing one of his favorite places. "I hadn't been doing my exercises."

"Why not?"

Oh, he just had to go for extra blood. Give Ferris an inch and he wanted a mile. "What sort of answer are you after? Let me know and I'll repeat it ad verbatim."

"Will you? That's unusually amenable of you."

"Says you."

"Here we are."

I'd been so intent on the conversation with Ferris that I hadn't been paying the slightest bit of attention to any of the exhibits we'd been passing. The large, red coded signs everywhere announced that we were in the Earth Hall, Ferris having brought me to a stop inside a mock-up of a shop, the signs and décor making it clear that it was meant to represent a place in Japan. "Ooh, a shop."

Ferris gave the wheelchair a little shake. "Wait!"

I waited, the floor starting to judder a few moments later, two children running around and squealing in delight as the effects kicked in.

Ferris leaned in over my shoulder, his breath tickling my cheek. "It's what an earthquake feels like. You probably get them all the time in Miami."

I turned my head toward him. Close enough to kiss again. I really needed to stop thinking about kissing him. "Actually, Miami isn't on a plate boundary so earthquakes there are extremely rare. Now, California is different, but luckily I've never been there during one."

"Huh! Well, geography never was my strong point." He waited until the floor had stopped shaking before wheeling me back out of the shop. "How do you feel about rocks?"

I pondered the strange question. "Erm... pretty neutral. I can't say they either excite me or instill a strong sense of rage, unless someone has thrown one at me and then that's a different matter. Are you going to throw rocks at me?"

"Not right at the moment." Ferris took a sharp right. "We'll skip rocks then and head to dinosaurs. It would take hours to cover the whole museum so I'm giving you a whistle-stop tour of all the best bits. Or at least what I think are the best bits." He plucked a map off a stand as we passed and flicked it onto my lap. "Have a look. Let me know if there's anything you particularly want to see."

I opened up the map, barely getting a couple of seconds to glance at it before we stopped in front of a large glass display case. "You know these aren't dinosaurs, right?"

Ferris snorted. "Ha, you're so funny! This is on the way to the dinosaurs. These are birds."

I smirked. "Well, thanks for clearing that up." There was every type of stuffed bird under the sun from vultures to humming birds. I wheeled myself closer to a display case where a male and female dodo were sharing space with a penguin.

Ferris leaned in to see what I was looking at. "It's not surprising they went extinct, is it? They're not exactly built for speed." He poked me in the shoulder. "Bit like you."

I gasped in outrage. "Are you seriously comparing a man with a fractured pelvis to an extinct and rather overweight bird?"

His reflection nodded. "I think I am. I reckon if you've got a problem with that, I can outrun you easily."

I huffed. "Anyway, they didn't go extinct because they couldn't run fast, they went extinct because they only lived on Mauritius and human settlers destroyed their habitat and then started eating them."

Ferris's eyes widened. "I'm impressed. You actually know some stuff."

It was almost tempting to leave him thinking that. Almost. But the short-term satisfaction of getting one over on him won out in the end. I pointed at the information by the dodo. "If you mean I can read, then yes, I've been doing it for quite a few years. I'm a very clever boy."

Ferris's lips twitched, but he didn't say anything, choosing to grab the handles of the wheelchair and steer me away from the display. For the next hour or so, I was treated to a tour which encompassed a display of stuffed mammals to match the birds, dinosaur skeletons, and an animatronic T-Rex which I had to admit was awe-inspiring and slightly terrifying at the same time, the crowds gathered to watch the attraction all seeming to feel the same way. I'd never found museums that interesting, but I'd never been to one with Ferris before, our constant banter as we tried to outdo each other ensuring that there was never a dull moment. And I had to admit—to myself anyway— that it was nice to get out of the house.

I was getting used to Ferris's abrupt stops, so I was quick to brace myself as we halted in front of the God-knows-how-many-feet-tall tree in the central hall, one of the baubles on a lower branch about an inch from my nose. I supposed I should be grateful I wasn't wearing the tree.

"Now, Xander, I want you to have a good look at this."

I frowned. "I can't see anything except bauble."

He reversed me a foot or so, the whole tree coming into view. "What am I looking at exactly?"

Ferris held up a finger. "I'm glad you asked. This"—he waved an arm up and down the length of the tree—"is Christmas." He elongated the word like he was speaking to a child. "See the decorations. That's what people do when they're not a long-lost relative of Ebenezer Scrooge. You too could have something like this in your home, something that represents the joy of the festive season."

I craned my neck so I could see the top of the tree. "It wouldn't fit. Not unless I removed the roof, and then the value of the house would go down quite considerably. Not to mention that the cost of my central heating would be astronomical from trying to heat it with a hole in the roof."

I was whisked away from the tree as quickly as we'd arrived at it. "How do you feel about old women?"

Had I misheard? After a minute's contemplation, I came to the conclusion I hadn't. "Is there a stuffed one of those here as well? Or are you suggesting I get one for the living room? I think there's rules against decorating old age pensioners, even at Christmas."

Ferris laughed. "I promised an ex-patient of mine that I'd drop in for tea some time. She lives near here, so I thought I'd kill two birds with one stone. But if you want to go straight home, we can do that. I can visit her some other time."

I shrugged. "Tea would be good." The idea of seeing Ferris interact with an actual patient—I still couldn't quite see myself as one—was too intriguing to pass up.

After the obligatory visit to the museum shop, Ferris insisting on buying me a T-Rex keyring that I had absolutely no use for, we left the museum.

CHAPTER TEN

Ferris

It had been a far more enjoyable day than I'd envisaged when I'd first come up with the idea of Operation Get Xander Out of the House. Of course he'd been resistant to getting in the wheelchair. I'd known he would be. And I'd known I'd be able to talk him into it. And of course, he'd tried to make out that he wasn't having a good time. God forbid Xander Cole let anyone see that he could get enjoyment out of something as simple as a museum. But even he hadn't been able to hide his fascination with some of the exhibits. I hadn't met a man—or woman—yet who could come face to face with a stuffed grizzly bear and not be impressed by its size.

I should probably have quit while I was ahead, but some demon in my head had demanded that I delay us getting back to the house for that little bit longer. If I was honest, it probably had a lot to do with Xander not even having mentioned his painkillers once. If this was what it took to wean him off them, then I was all for it.

Therefore, we were on our way to pay an impromptu visit to Mrs. Brown, who may or may not even be at home. I knew she'd been discharged from the hospital the previous week, but there was no guarantee that she wasn't already back there. I wheeled Xander up the garden path, the house not offering any clues as to whether it was occupied or not. I guessed there was only one way to find out, Xander remaining silent as I raised my hand to knock.

There was a very long wait before the door eventually opened, Mrs. Brown looking even tinier than she normally did on the doorstep. Her smile was immediate. "Ferris!"

I smiled back at her. "Surprise! I promised I'd drop round for tea, didn't I? I hope it's okay that I've brought a friend?"

Mrs. Brown's gaze dropped to Xander, as if she hadn't actually noticed him before I'd mentioned him. She definitely noticed him now, though, her gaze staying on him for far longer than it needed to. *Good looking bastard.* Her smile grew even wider. "That's absolutely fine. The more the merrier. Come in."

She stood aside and I maneuvered Xander over the step and in the direction of the room that Mrs. Brown had indicated, which turned out to be the kitchen. I parked him underneath the kitchen table, his gaze traveling to the ornate Christmas centerpiece made up of holly, white roses, gold baubles, and matching candles. Xander narrowed his eyes at me. "Don't say it."

Mrs. Brown's brow furrowed. "Don't say what?"

I placed my hand on Xander's shoulder, the muscles tightening beneath my fingers. "Xander's allergic to Christmas. He breaks out in hives if anything Christmassy gets too close to him."

"Oh really?" Mrs. Brown's expression said that she was truly sad for him. "I love Christmas. When you get to my age, you have to have something to look forward to. I love everything about it, the decorations, the carols, the traditions." Her expression turned wistful. "I do miss going to midnight mass, but everything else I can still do."

She turned her attention to Xander. "What is it about Christmas that upsets you so much?"

Xander aimed a glare my way, and I was forced to turn away to hide my smirk.

He smiled at Mrs. Brown. "Christmas doesn't upset me in the slightest. Ferris has a rather overactive imagination just because my house isn't lit up like Madison Square Garden." He gestured at the wheelchair. "I'm in this because I'm recovering from a fractured pelvis, but Ferris would still have me up a stepladder hanging ceiling decorations, just so he could ooh and aah at them."

"Not quite true." I gestured for Mrs. Brown to sit as she made as if to start making tea. There was no way I was going to let an eighty-year-old wait on me.

She took a seat at the table next to Xander with a grateful smile. "You're a very sweet boy, Ferris."

My "I know" was all but drowned out by Xander's snort.

I set about locating cups as Mrs. Brown chatted to Xander in the background. "He's my favorite nurse."

Xander coughed. "Oh really. Mine too." I raised an eyebrow at that one, but I should have known there was a punchline coming, and he didn't disappoint. "Mind, I only know one so the competition isn't that fierce."

Mrs. Brown laughed. "You're such a joker. How do you two know each other? Have you been dating long?"

I nearly swallowed my own tongue at that one. It was lucky I was facing the cupboard. Although, as the silence went on for that beat too long, I was tempted to turn around to see what expression Xander was wearing.

He finally answered the question. "We're not dating."

I didn't like those words, which was stupid when they were the truth.

"Oh?" Mrs. Brown sounded confused.

I added teabags to the cups while I pretended not to be listening. I doubted it was that convincing when I was less than a meter away.

"My brother hired him to look after me while he was away for Christmas. He didn't think I could manage on my own, which was utter..." I smiled as Xander censored himself. "...rubbish. I would have been just fine on my own. Our... relationship is strictly professional."

Did he need to sound so sure about that? What about all the flirting? Not to mention the way I caught him looking at me sometimes. And he'd definitely checked me out when I'd only been dressed in a towel. Purely professional, my arse.

"I see." Mrs. Brown cleared her throat. "I hope you don't mind me asking, but you are gay though, aren't you?"

The kettle finished boiling as Xander assured her that he was. By that time, I couldn't delay carrying everything over to the table without it looking like I'd gained a strange fascination for Mrs. Brown's kitchen wall. I frowned as Mrs. Brown produced a photo out of nowhere and pushed it in front of Xander. She glanced my way as I deposited the cups on the table. "Biscuits are in the top cupboard, Ferris." I obediently turned back to get them, finding an unopened variety pack. Mrs. Brown tapped her finger on the photo. "The handsome young man in the middle is my grandson, Brandon. He's about your age. I could introduce you."

Xander politely leaned forward to get a better look. I shook my head as I took a seat at the kitchen table. There I was, thinking that Mrs. Brown's enthusiasm for playing matchmaker had been about her concern for me being single. It turned out it was nothing of the sort. She was just determined to completely rewrite her grandson's sexuality. I reached over to lay a finger on the smiling, blonde woman in the photo that Brandon had his arm around. "That's his wife. They've been married for five years." I trailed my finger lower to the two children posing in front of the couple. "And that's their kids, a four-year-old, and a two-year-old."

Mrs. Brown made a pfft sound. She tugged the photo away from my hand and pushed it more firmly in front of Xander. "Ferris already turned him down."

Xander lifted his head and met my gaze, his eyes shining with amusement. "Is that so? What's wrong with him, Ferris?"

I rolled my eyes at him. "You mean apart from the wife and kids?"

Xander's smile was full of evil intent. "Isn't that heterophobic?"

I sat back and crossed my arms over my chest. "That's me, a great big screaming heterophobe."

Mrs. Brown reached over to open the biscuits. "Brandon can speak Japanese."

I laughed. "Can he? There you go, Xander. Fancy hearing 'what are you doing here? Get out of my bed before I call the police' in Japanese?"

We both laughed and for a minute there was no Mrs. Brown. There was only the two of us. I liked Xander Cole, and I had a feeling that keeping things purely professional was going to be a lot harder than I'd originally envisaged.

·♥·♥·♥·♥·♥·

About an hour into our visit with Mrs. Brown—who by that time had announced that we should both call her Dorothy—Xander had started looking decidedly pale and strained. I'd immediately brought things to a close and called a cab, so that our journey back would be much quicker. Luckily, the wheelchair was one that folded up.

Back at the house, I hadn't even tried to talk Xander out of it when he'd taken a painkiller and gone straight to bed. It had left me alone in the living room, flicking through TV programs I had little interest in watching in an effort to kill time.

In the end, I gave into the inevitable and called my mum. We'd only had one conversation since I'd walked out on her without an explanation, and that had been decidedly curt, my mum not understanding my sudden U-turn when I still wasn't prepared to drop Barry in it by telling her the real reason. It had left us at an awkward impasse, an awkward impasse I'd been doing my best to ignore. But it was either that or watch a gardening program, and since I didn't even have a flat, never mind a garden, it wasn't much of a choice.

It rang for so long that I was resigned to it going to voicemail when she finally picked up with a breathless "hello."

I put it on speakerphone. "Hey mum. I just thought I'd see how you were, and let you know how the new job is going."

"I'm good. Everything is fine. I still don't understand why you made such a big deal of taking a month off and then ended up agreeing to work anyway."

I sighed at the fact we hadn't even managed one minute of small talk. "You know why. It came with a place to stay, which was something I was distinctly short of at the time."

"You had a place to stay."

I knew my mum and I knew that if I didn't change the subject, we would go round in circles until I was forced to end the conversation or risk losing my sanity.

"Aren't you going to ask me how it's going?"

There was a long pause before my mum grudgingly asked, "How's it going?"

I lounged back on the sofa. "The house is lovely. My room's small, but the bed is comfy. It's not exactly a hardship to stay here."

"And what about the patient?"

"Xander? Well, Xander is… Xander."

"What does he do for a living that he can manage to own his own house in that area?"

"He's a model."

"A model?"

"Yes Mum, a model. Some people are."

"Do you remember what happened with that other model?"

I winced. "Do you mean Jack?"

"How many other models have you dated?"

"None that I know of, but I don't tend to interrogate people and check on absolutely everything they've ever done from the moment they were born. Some of them probably had paper rounds as a kid that I never knew about."

"Jack cheated on you."

"Yeah, thanks for that reminder. I remember it vividly." I did. It was hard to forget discovering the fact that your boyfriend had had another boyfriend all along, one that he'd had zero intentions of giving up. Apparently one man hadn't been enough for Jack. He'd wanted to have his cake and eat it. The worst of it was that he'd seemed perturbed by my annoyance, telling me that that was just the way things worked in the circles he mixed in.

"Why didn't you want to stay here?"

I swore under my breath, quiet enough that my mum wouldn't be able to hear it. I lifted my head to find a silent shadow in the doorway. How long had Xander been standing there? I must have been deaf not to have heard him clonking down the stairs on his crutches. Stealthy, he certainly wasn't. Not unless an elephant could ever be classed as stealthy. His presence provided me with the perfect excuse to end the call, though. "I have to go, Mum. Xander is up from his nap and I need to… do medical things."

Xander's eyebrows shot up at that, and it was all I could do not to laugh as I quickly brought the conversation to a close before my mum could protest. Xander watched me closely until he was sure that I'd ended the call. "What medical things? It's nothing kinky, is it? Because I've got to tell you that, although I like to think of myself as pretty cosmopolitan, medical kink is not high on the list of things I'd be up for. In fact, I'm pretty sure it's bottom of the list."

"So you're up for fisting?"

Xander blinked as he maneuvered himself over to the sofa, abandoning his crutches as he eased himself onto it. "As I was saying, it comes just above fisting on my list of sexual experiences I never intend to try."

I laughed, my mirth short-lived as I was suddenly skewered by a green gaze. "Why didn't you just tell her?"

I didn't need to ask what Xander was referring to. It was obvious. And it was a good question. One I'd asked myself more than a few times. "Because… she's happy. Why would I want to ruin that? If I tell her, what's going to happen?" It was a rhetorical question so I didn't wait for an answer. "There's only two possible outcomes. She believes me and she dumps him and then she's miserable because she thought she was having this great relationship and it's turned to shit. Or she doesn't believe me and then the relationship between the two of us is ruined until she finally finds out one day that I was telling the truth after all. It's a lose/lose situation."

Xander grimaced. "I suppose. It just seems crap that you can't tell her, and meanwhile whatshisname…"

He paused and I provided the name he was searching for. "Barry."

"Yeah, meanwhile Barry gets to be a sleazebag. Does she even know he's into guys?"

I shrugged. "I have no idea. You'd hope they might have had that conversation, but it's not like I discuss my mum's sex life with her, thank God. If she ever tried to, I'd probably shrivel up and die." I gave a dramatic shudder. In a bid to get off the subject, I scrutinized Xander. He looked like he always did when he'd taken painkillers, like he'd gone one step forward and two steps back, the dark shadows under his eyes not giving the impression that he'd spent the last few hours sleeping. It made me feel bad. "I'm sorry, I pushed you too far today. We should have come straight home after the museum. Your home, I mean. Visiting Dorothy should have waited for another day."

Xander shrugged. "I don't mind. Dorothy was… interesting. Why is she so keen for her grandson to be gay anyway?"

I grinned at him. "Well, that's the million-dollar question, isn't it? Who knows how Dorothy Brown's brain works? I certainly don't."

Xander leaned his head back against the sofa and closed his eyes. I had to fight the urge to pull his head against my shoulder and encourage him to rest there. Jesus! I was going soft. Well, apart from one part of my anatomy, which was trying to go in completely the opposite direction. What would he do if I did pull him over to me? Would he push me off? Or would he stay there? My fingers itched to find out. Should I? I could always pass it off as a friendly gesture. It wasn't like it was a proposal of marriage.

Xander suddenly sat up with a start, his gaze narrowing on the TV screen. "Are you watching a gardening program?"

I didn't answer. It was plainly obvious from the discussion of what pH the soil needed to be for optimum growth of begonias that it was indeed a gardening program. I supposed I should be glad that it had ruined what could have been a moment of absolute madness.

CHAPTER ELEVEN

Xander

December 13th

I lowered the book I was reading, eying Ferris suspiciously as he pored over the laptop he'd asked to borrow. He hadn't told me what he wanted it for, and I hadn't asked. Only now I wished I had. A quiet Ferris wasn't a good Ferris. A quiet Ferris either meant he was up to something, or there was something going on in his head he didn't want me to know about. Life was noisier but far safer when he was talking.

It had been nearly two weeks since he'd exploded into my life, and apart from yesterday's enjoyable but tiring expedition, we'd fallen into a surprisingly domestic routine. I hadn't admitted as much to him, but the exercises really were helping, my mobility getting a little easier each day, which in turn had started to make the exercises less painful. Although, Ferris always seemed to find something else to add just to fuck with me. I was beginning to think he was making some of the exercises up. The day I found myself balancing on one leg while holding a tin of beans in each hand I was going to cry foul.

I'd cut down on the painkillers. Ferris might not comment, but his disapproving stare spoke volumes. Besides, the afternoon naps left me feeling worse than when I'd gone to sleep in the first place.

I tested that old adage that if you stared at someone for long enough, they'd notice. Apparently, Ferris was immune. I tried narrowing my eyes and turning it into more of a glare. Still oblivious. Either he was ignoring me on purpose, or whatever was on screen was far more fascinating than I was. I coughed. Still nothing. Frustration had me closing the book I'd been reading and focusing all my attention on him, which was more than I could say for him. I gave brief thought to rolling off the sofa in a dead faint. Only, it would hurt. A lot. And there was no guarantee it would garner any reaction from him whatsoever. One thing I'd learned about Ferris was that he was only a nurse when it suited him.

There was only one thing for it. I'd have to go for an actual question. "What are you looking at?"

A slow smile spread across his face, but he still didn't bother to look up. "You!"

"What?"

He turned the laptop screen around so that I could see the picture on the screen. It was indeed me, the photo from a catwalk show I'd done in Milan, one where I was wearing a cream jacket with no shirt underneath. I only caught a quick glimpse of it before he turned the screen back to face him, leaning closer as if he needed to inspect something.

It was a weird feeling to discover that the person whose attention I'd been competing with was—me. It was also a weird feeling not to have a clue what was so interesting about the photo. He made a noise in his throat before clicking the mouse.

"You asked to borrow the laptop to Google me?"

He pulled a face. "Hardly. Get over yourself. I needed to send an important email without fiddling about on my phone and accidentally saying something I didn't mean to. *Then* I Googled you while I happened to be online."

"I stand corrected."

He peered at me over the top of the screen. "You can barely stand. You might want to choose a different saying."

"Bitch."

"Takes one to know one."

I smothered a smile, doing my best to hide how much I enjoyed our constant war of words. "*Why* did you Google me?"

Another glance. "I wanted to see what you looked like in proper clothes."

I glanced down at my ubiquitous sweatpants and T-shirt. "I look the same, but smarter."

He let out a snort. "In your dreams."

"Alright, the same, but with make-up on, and hair that's been teased into submission by a team of highly skilled personnel for hours on end, who go into a cold sweat if a hair manages to express some degree of personal freedom."

Ferris's lips curled into a smile. "That's more like it."

"I could take offense."

He spared me a glance. "Feel free."

"You do know that mental health is very important to recovery. Your comments are probably putting me back weeks."

He shook his head. "I didn't say you looked better in the photos. You're jumping to that conclusion all on your own." He tilted his head to one side, as if trying to get a different view on something. I had a horrible suspicion that he'd stumbled over the underwear campaign I'd done. The thought of him looking at my barely clad body did strange things to me. "What are you looking at now?"

"Nothing."

"Show me."

"You want to look at yourself? Narcissist! Want me to bring you a mirror so that you can stare at yourself to your heart's content? Maybe I could print some photos for you, so that you can surround yourself with them. I bet that's why you didn't want me to stay with you. You wanted to spend Christmas with just you and yourself, didn't you?"

"Dick."

He clicked the mouse again. "Who's that?"

He turned the screen around again and I stared at the picture of myself and Harvey. It had been taken a few months back when he'd dragged me to a party on the beach. We both looked happy and at ease in the photo. That had changed a couple of hours after the photo had been taken, happiness giving way to a blazing row when Harvey had gotten a little too close to the party host for my liking. He'd sworn that nothing had happened, but I'd drawn my own conclusions about finding them alone in a bedroom, both of them far more rumpled than the last time I'd seen them. It wasn't the first time I'd had doubts about Harvey's fidelity, but just like every other time, I'd let him convince me that it was simply my own paranoia at play. "Harvey Walker. He's a photographer. I'm surprised you haven't heard of him."

Ferris grimaced. "I don't exactly move in those circles. The only photographer I know is Harry. He did a friend's wedding for half price. Good photos. Let me know if you ever fall on hard times and need to downgrade." He turned the screen back, continuing to browse. I watched him, seeing the moment where something gave him pause. "I'm guessing he's not just a photographer to you. Unless you like to thank all your photographers by tonguing them enthusiastically. If so, my phone has a camera, we should take some shots. You know, for… medical purposes."

"Harvey's my… boyfriend…" I hastily corrected myself. "Ex-boyfriend. Yeah, ex-boyfriend, I think…"

"You think?"

Ferris's voice was heavy with scorn. I didn't blame him. I'd sounded less than convincing. But the truth was we hadn't had any big break-up scene, so it wasn't that clear cut. "Well, he's not here, and he's not answering any of my calls, and he left about five minutes after I had the accident."

For a moment Ferris's gaze was sharp and assessing as he focused on me. It only lasted a few seconds until his eyes softened and he was back to being the man I was more used to seeing, the one who was funny, caring, and witty. The man who'd proven he could get under my skin in all the best ways and was growing on me so quickly it was scary.

Spending all day together within the confines of my house meant we already knew an awful lot about each other. I hadn't mentioned Harvey because I hadn't felt like I needed to. Ferris leaned forward, resting his chin on his hand and holding my gaze. "This Harvey guy sounds like a complete idiot. You can do better."

I stared back at him, trying to make it look like I wasn't staring at his lips when I was. It was his fault my mind had wandered down that road again. He was the one who'd just joked about me thanking people by tonguing them enthusiastically. Well, I had a lot to thank Ferris for, and I was happy to start whenever he was ready. "Yeah, I'm beginning to think I can."

Ferris broke the moment by walking over to the window to stare out. "It's snowing."

"Yeah?" I heaved myself to my feet, grabbing my crutches and making my slow way over to join him. At least the pain was more of a dull throb than a screaming cacophony now. He was right; it was snowing. Not tiny flakes either, but huge great ones that were already settling on the paving stones. I stood deliberately close to him as we watched, pretending that the crutches meant I needed the support when it was more about enjoying the body heat coming off him. "I hate snow."

I felt, more than heard the sigh from Ferris, his shoulder moving against mine in a gesture that was easy to interpret. "Way to spoil the pretty moment, dude. I thought I might get to enjoy the rare sight of snow in London for longer than a minute before Mr. Negative blundered in and ruined it. What have you got against snow exactly?"

I twisted myself around so that I could look him in the eye. "Seriously?" Given that my hands were wrapped around the crutches and I had no wish to fall to the floor like a dying swan, I had to use my chin to indicate my body—an action that probably made it look more like I'd had a funny turn. "I wouldn't be in this state if it weren't for snow."

Ferris's lips twitched as if he was struggling to keep a straight face. "You're blaming the snow for your accident?"

"Well, if it hadn't been there, I would have been fine."

"If it hadn't been there, you would have looked really stupid skiing."

He had a point. "Alright, I hate skiing, which only happens because there's snow, so I still feel like snow has to take at least some of the blame."

I was rewarded with what was becoming a customary Ferris eye roll for that comment. At least, I didn't have to suffer it for too long, given he was already heading away from the window to go... Actually, I didn't have a clue where he was going. "What are you doing?"

At the sound of the front door opening without an answer from him, I sighed, resigning myself to another trek to the door. When I got there, it was to find it wide open, Ferris standing outside with his face tipped up to the sky. He seemed oblivious to the fact that he was only wearing a T-shirt. Snowflakes glittered in his hair, making him look like some sort of snow fairy sent down from heaven. He spread his arms out wide, turning round in a slow circle. I let out another sigh. "You're getting wet."

"I love snow!"

"Of course you do. You love everything. Why should snow be any different?"

He turned with a grin. "Come outside."

I regarded him silently, trying to push down the constant feeling that kept rearing its head, that little voice inside me that kept telling me how much I was growing to like him, how much I liked him being there. *I want to kiss you.* "I don't think that's a good idea with crutches."

"You'll be fine."

I really want to kiss you. "Is that your considered medical opinion?"

His grin widened, his brown eyes twinkling. "If you like. If you fall, I'll catch you. Promise."

I'd also be happy to lick each and every snowflake from your body should you require that service. I promise to do a very thorough job. "You'll catch your death, and then I'll end up having to nurse you instead."

He laughed. "I'd be dead within the week."

"Exactly. So, you should come inside."

"You should come outside, and *then* I'll come inside."

If the last however many days with this man had taught me anything, it was that he wasn't one to back down. Therefore, it was simpler just to get it over with. Before all the heat that had been in my house permanently took up residence outside. Luckily, there was only one step to navigate, Ferris doing absolutely nothing to help as I navigated it with the crutches until I was stood next to him, freezing particles of snow immediately starting to melt against my skin. "Well, here I am... outside. Time to go in."

"Two minutes."

"You keep changing the rules."

He grabbed my arm as if he thought I might try and escape, turning me to face him. "Tell me that it's not that bad. Tell me that under that grumpy exterior, you like the feel of the snow against your face, that it makes you feel alive. Tell me something good."

You're gorgeous. Except, I couldn't tell him that. I couldn't tell him that my burning need to kiss him was growing exponentially hour by hour either, and I couldn't tell him that I wasn't sure how much longer I could hold off if he kept on looking at me the way he was. I couldn't even see the snow. All I could see was him. And *he* was beautiful. It was quite the situation I'd found myself in.

CHAPTER TWELVE

Ferris

I'd come to a decision. We were halfway through December with Christmas just around the corner, and Xander still hadn't shown the slightest bit of interest in embracing the festive season. It might be his house, but I had to live here too. Therefore, it was time to do something about it. I'd start off slow, gauge his reaction and then see how far I could push it.

With Xander still in bed, I made a quick phone call, taking delivery of the first item within the hour. A floorboard creaked above my head and I just had time to shove the item where I'd decided it would look best, which happened to be the corner of the living room before the familiar *tap tap* of Ferris's crutches came down the stairs.

Knowing that Xander was a creature of habit and would head to the kitchen first, I stayed in the living room. His excursion wouldn't last long once he realized that my dastardly plan to bring Christmas to the Cole household had prevented me from even thinking about breakfast.

"Ferris?"

I smiled at the fact that the call had come within about five seconds of him reaching the kitchen. "Yeah?"

"Who was at the door?"

"No one."

"So I was woken by a doorbell that only existed in my head. Is that what you're telling me?"

"Probably."

There was a long pause. "What happened to breakfast?"

Xander sounded decidedly grumpy. Or should that be even more grumpy than usual. "I'll get right on that, sir. Very sorry, sir. Unfortunately, I was unable to calculate your exact time of getting out of bed with any reliable degree of accuracy."

The thump of crutches came down the hallway and I braced myself. Xander's gaze was fixed on the floor as he came into the room. It was for that reason that he failed to notice the new addition until he was almost on top of it. He blinked a few times. "What the hell is that?"

I divested him of his crutches, propping him against the back of the sofa before sliding my arm around his neck, unable to resist playing with the hair at the nape of his neck. "That, my friend, is a Christmas tree. A tradition thought to have been started by the Germans back in the 16th century when devout Christians brought decorated trees into their home. No home is complete now without one at Christmas. Well, unless you don't celebrate Christmas for religious reasons of course. Do you remember we saw one in the Natural History Museum? I made a special effort to point one out to you because that's the kind of generous person I am."

He stared at me. "I know what the fuck it is. What's it doing in my living room?"

"Then you asked the wrong question. Your question should have been—"

Xander's glare was particularly venomous, stopping me in mid flow. I let out a weary sigh. I hadn't expected him to be overjoyed, but at the end of the day it was just a tree. It was a good tree as well, one that was at least seven-foot tall. I'd been extremely lucky to get hold of it at such short notice. "I thought it would be nice. Bring a bit of festive cheer to the place."

Xander shifted his glare to the tree, as if it was supposed to share some of the blame simply for existing. "Just what I need. One more thing to trip over."

I frowned. Now, that was an argument I wasn't going to accept. "It's in the corner. Unless you were planning on walking into the wall, I can't see how you can trip over it."

Xander looked like he was gearing up to prove that he could if only to prove a point. He snatched the crutches back off me and made his way over to the window, his demeanor that of a man who was unhappy about far more than a tree.

"What's up?"

It was his turn to sigh. "I don't know. I guess I keep thinking about what I'd normally be doing at this time of year."

I joined him at the window. "Which is?"

He shrugged. "Different stuff. Last year I was on a yacht in the middle of the Mediterranean Sea."

"And this year, you're stuck here with me."

Xander's lips twitched. "That part is not the problem."

I feigned mock shock. "Did you just pay me a compliment?" I clasped a hand to my chest. "That's so sweet, that you would rather be here with me than on a yacht."

"I don't remember saying that."

"But's that what you meant."

Something fluttered in my chest when he didn't bother to deny it. It made me want to please him rather than pissing him off. "Do you want me to get rid of it?" I wasn't great at hiding my disappointment.

Xander cast a quick glance back to the tree, his gaze raking it from head to toe. "You were going to decorate it, right? It wasn't just going to sit there like that?"

I strode over to the large cardboard box that had been delivered at the same time as the tree, lifting it and giving it a shake. "Decorations!"

Xander's gaze darted between me and the tree. "I guess it's up now. It might as well stay. It's just a tree."

I grinned at him. "We can decorate it after breakfast."

Xander's eyebrows shot up. "We?"

I placed the box on the floor. "Of course. Surely, you don't trust me on my own with such an important job. Imagine what horrendous things I might add to it when you're not looking."

"That's a very good point. I need to at least supervise."

I couldn't help feeling like I'd won an important victory. Not only had I convinced Xander to let a little Christmas into his life, but I'd managed to get him to agree to help. He wasn't to know that by conceding the battle, the war had only just begun. Xander probably thought I'd be happy with a tree. Well, he didn't know me that well if he thought that. By the time I'd finished with him, he was going to be drenched in Christmas. And if it kept me busy and stopped me from dwelling on the rather nice photos of Xander that I'd insisted on torturing myself by finding online, then all the better.

·♥·♥·♥·♥·♥·

I'd set Xander up on a chair in front of the tree, informing him that he was going to decorate the bottom while I did the top. He'd grumbled about it, but I'd taken him sitting there as agreement. Opening the mystery box of decorations revealed plain fairy lights, purple and silver baubles, white snowman and snowflakes, and silver tinsel. While I would have probably chosen something a little more unusual, the fact Xander hadn't managed to find something to complain about meant they must have passed muster.

I took charge of winding the fairy lights around the tree, treating Xander to a rousing rendition of "Good King Wenceslas" while he sat and watched.

"Is that necessary?"

"The fairy lights?"

"No, not the… fricking fairy lights, the musical accompaniment."

"Very necessary. It gets us in the mood."

"The mood for what?"

Happy with their positioning, I flicked the switch to test them, smiling when they all obediently flickered to life. "The mood for Christmas."

Xander made a noise that said he wasn't quite there yet.

"Perhaps that song's not working for you." I launched into a version of "O Little Town of Bethlehem." Granted it had been years since I last heard the song, so there was a certain amount of artistic license involved in some of the lyrics. Even so, Xander covering his ears with his hands was just plain rude. I dangled a snowman ornament above his ear until it annoyed him enough to swipe at it.

He craned his head back to look up at me. "Stop it."

Smiling innocently, I passed him the ornament. "Just trying to provide you with the things you need to decorate."

Xander snatched it from me. "Yeah? Well, funnily enough, my ears have never gained the ability to grasp objects."

"No? That's disappointing. I thought you were multi-talented."

He shoved the ornament on the closest branch to him and I passed him another. It ended up on an adjacent branch to the first one.

"Seriously?"

He shrugged. "What?"

I sighed. "You have to spread them out. You can't stick all the snowmen together, like it's some sort of snowman convention. It's like you've never decorated a tree before."

"I haven't."

Huh! What kind of person had never decorated a tree? I guess one who spent most of the year gallivanting around exotic places and was never in one place long enough to bother about such domestic things. "What about when you were a kid? You must have at least helped then?"

Xander shook his head. "My parents used to buy one of those already decorated ones."

"Urgh! That's sacrilege."

Xander rolled his eyes. "Let me guess, your house was one of those decorated inside and out, where the lights were so bright you were at risk of being blinded."

"Not quite. My dad died when I was little, so Christmas was mostly just me and my mum. We had a tree, but that was about it. She was always really sad around Christmas."

Xander went quiet and I grimaced. So much for creating a festive mood. I'd just covered it in a thick layer of depression. What was I going to do for an encore, dress in Victorian clothes and beg for more food? "It was fine, and it was a long time ago."

Xander moved the ornament to another branch so that the two snowmen had a sizeable gap between them. "That explains a lot."

I deposited some more snowmen in Xander's lap, my fingers inadvertently brushing his thigh. "About what?"

"Why you won't tell your mum that her boyfriend is a sleaze. You've seen enough of her being sad to last you a lifetime."

I added a snowman to one of the higher branches. "Probably." I couldn't say that I was a fan of having Xander Cole psychoanalyze me. Especially when he was probably right. It called for another song. I launched into one with gusto. "Siiiilent night. Hoooooly night. All is caaaaaalm. All is briiiiight." Xander made a noise like a chicken slowly being strangled, but I carried on regardless. "Round yon vi-ir-gin, mother and child. Holy infant so tender and mild." Xander should be grateful I knew the words to this one. So far, anyway.

"Not many virgins round here."

I stopped mid high note. "Xander Cole…" I needed to find out his middle name. Full naming someone worked far better when you knew the entire thing. "Is this your way of admitting to being a slut? Is that how things work in the modeling world? Is it a non-stop whirlwind of orgies and partner swapping?" I'd phrased it as a joke, but I was genuinely interested in the answer.

Finding out that he and Harvey Walker were an item, or had been an item, had come as a bit of a shock. It wasn't like I'd fooled myself into thinking that Xander didn't have any relationships in his past, but knowing it and seeing photographic proof of it splashed across the internet were very different things. The two of them certainly hadn't been shy about puckering up for the camera. And Xander had looked happy. It had been a much-needed reminder that Xander's life and mine were poles apart. It was far too easy to forget that when you were holed up in a house together.

"Hardly."

I'd been so lost in thought that it took a moment to remember what question he was answering. Right—orgies and partner swapping. "No? I would have thought that anything goes." Snowmen all on the tree, I passed half of the snowflakes to my reluctant decorating partner, who I had to admit had fallen into line after my revelation about my childhood.

Xander pulled a face. "It probably does for some people. But I'm not, nor have I ever been, one of those people. One man's enough for me."

"What about Harvey?"

Xander paused in his placement of a snowflake to shoot me a quizzical look. "What about him?"

Yeah, what about him indeed? What was I hoping Xander was going to say? Was I hoping he was going to tell me that he was a complete shithead? I shrugged. "Just curious, I guess. How long were you together?"

Xander looked pained. "Define together."

I hid my frown behind the pretense of pondering exactly where the snowflake in my hand needed to go. "I didn't realize it was that difficult a question."

"Yeah, well." Xander exhaled noisily. "I guess it is. Do you mind if we don't talk about Harvey?"

I turned the tree round so that we could add some snowflakes to the back. "It's either that or Christmas songs. The choice is yours."

"Oh God. What a choice. That's like asking me if I want to put vinegar or lemon juice in my eye."

I laughed. "Which would you go for?"

"Neither. I'm not a weirdo. I bet that you've got an answer, though."

I thought about it. "Vinegar."

"Why?"

"I've had lemon juice in my eye and it hurt like hell. I'd be stupid to pick something that I already know would hurt. Whereas vinegar is more of an unknown quantity. I might suspect it hurts just as much as lemon juice, but I don't know that until I've tried it. Therefore, I can be optimistic that it's not as bad right up until the moment of truth."

Xander accepted a handful of silver baubles from me. "There's some vinegar in the kitchen."

"I'll pass, thanks." I added a few baubles of my own. I had to admit that the tree was starting to look good. "Anyway, stop changing the subject, what Christmas song do you want? I take requests."

"I don't know. Something a little more modern maybe, that wasn't written hundreds of years before either of us were born."

"I can do modern." I cleared my throat dramatically. "Driving home for Christmas, with a thousand memories." I stopped. Far too miserable. We'd already done sad childhood Christmases and ex-boyfriends. We needed something a little more upbeat. "Laaast Christmas, you gave me your…" Too soppy.

I channeled my best Mariah Carey. "All I want for Christmas is you." Jesus! Definitely not the right song to be singing to Xander. Not when there was starting to be a ring of truth to it. Why were so many modern Christmas songs about love and relationships, anyway? I almost threw the purple baubles at Xander, thankful that my position behind him meant that he couldn't see the slight flush that had heated my cheeks.

Xander tipped his head to one side. "That's an interesting medley. I've never heard those three songs spliced together before, and I've got to tell you that I won't be at all sad if I never hear it again."

"You just don't appreciate good music."

"Oh, I appreciate *good* music, just not whatever that was."

I added the tinsel, switched the lights on again and then stood back to admire our handiwork. "What do you think?"

Xander gave the tree careful consideration. "I think…" I braced myself for a cutting comment. "I think it looks good." He smiled. "Although, the bottom of the tree is clearly much better than the top."

I snorted. "If it is, its only because of my intervention. Left to your own devices, we would have had separate zones for each ornament."

Xander turned to smile at me. "I might have started a new trend."

I found myself lost in the green of his eyes for a moment. They really were very pretty. I dragged my gaze away reluctantly. "You can do your exercises beneath the Christmas tree. It'll give you something to stare at when you're laid on your back."

"Great!"

Xander couldn't have sounded any less excited by the prospect.

CHAPTER THIRTEEN

Xander

December 15th

A family of reindeer had moved in overnight. Not a small family either. I'd reached twenty-two at my last count, and I wasn't entirely convinced I hadn't missed any. The only room that seemed to have escaped their hooved presence was my bedroom, which was a good job, because the thought of Ferris tiptoeing around it while I was asleep gave me a strange feeling in my gut, and in other places if I was honest. There was even a reindeer in the bathroom, its beady black eyes seeming very unimpressed with what it saw as it watched me take a piss. I had no idea where Ferris had gotten them from, and I'd decided I wasn't going to ask. In fact, I refused to give him the satisfaction of even mentioning them at all.

He took a bite of sausage, chewing it as he stared at me. "Do you like them?"

I pasted the most innocent look on my face that I could manage. "Sausages?"

"Reindeer."

I forked up a mouthful of scrambled egg, Ferris keeping to his side of the deal and cooking breakfast every morning as a reward for my diligence in completing my physio exercises. "I have no strong feelings about them one way or the other."

"I love reindeer."

"I'm sure they're fond of you too."

He regarded me silently across the table. Sometimes he looked at me in a way that said there was far more than just friendship between us. Or maybe I was just seeing what I wanted to see? "Where did you get them from?"

Ferris fluttered his eyelashes at me. "The sausages?"

I skewered him with a glare. "The reindeer."

"Oh, so you can see them." He stuck out his thumb and little finger and held it to his ear. "Hi. It's me again. I'd like to cancel that eye test that I booked earlier for a Mr. Cole. It seems that although there are many other things we need to work on, he does at least have slight vision. You don't happen to do a stubbornness test, do you? No?" He tutted. "That's a shame. I could do with one of those for him. Please do let me know if you ever implement one. He would make a perfect guinea pig. Yes, he'll come quietly. I have access to strong drugs."

I crossed my arms and waited for Ferris to run out of steam. "I might be able to see, but I'm regretting not being deaf at the moment. And is there any chance of you answering the question?"

Ferris tipped his head to one side. "What question?"

My lips twitched, but I refused to give him the satisfaction of smiling. "Where you got the reindeer from."

"What reindeer?"

"Ferris!"

He picked up a bright pink reindeer from the floor and placed it in the middle of the table. It was so big that if I wanted to keep Ferris in my eyeline, I was left with only two options: flatten myself to the table so I could see between its legs, or lean drunkenly to one side so I could see round it. I went for the latter, catching sight of him again as he smiled evilly. "Oh, *this* reindeer. I borrowed them from a friend. Don't worry. I left him some."

"How many did he have?" I was imagining a house jampacked full of reindeer. What sort of friends did Ferris have? I was starting to believe his story of being out on the streets if I hadn't let him stay. It wasn't surprising his friends wouldn't have had room if they filled them full of strange items.

Ferris shrugged. "I don't know. Who counts reindeer? That would be weird." He sat back in his chair. "They need names."

I forked up the last mouthful of egg. "Of course they do."

·♥·♥·♥·♥·♥·

The doorbell rang mid-afternoon. I lifted my head to stare at Ferris. He stared back. The doorbell rang again. I inclined my head in the direction of the door. "Are you going to get that?"

Ferris quirked an eyebrow. "Oh, so now you want me to get the door? When I pointed out that very thing, who was it who was singularly unimpressed by the idea? And in case that question is too hard for you, I'll provide the answer. That, my dear friend, was you. I'm a nurse not a butler."

"You'd look good in a butler's uniform." He would. But then Ferris could probably carry anything off.

He frowned. "Is that a kink of yours? You're not going to try and dress me up like a French maid, are you?"

I screwed my face up into something that hopefully looked convincing. "No!"

The doorbell rang again.

Ferris crossed his arms over his chest. "You're much more mobile now. Thanks to me."

My snort was perhaps a bit louder than it needed to be. "Thanks to you. I think it's probably got more to do with time. You know what they say, time is a great healer."

"Bollocks!"

I smiled, Ferris refusing to return it. I smiled wider. His lips twitched. He narrowed his eyes. "Would it kill you to admit that I was right?"

"I…" My phone rang and I grabbed it eagerly, the screen flashing up the name 'Mia.' Mia was a fellow model I'd met while on a shoot in Paris. We'd gotten on like a house on fire almost immediately despite her constant need for drama. If there wasn't any, she'd usually go out of her way to create some. I answered it with a smile. "Hi darling."

Ferris's head jerked up. What was eating him?

"Xan, sweetheart. Where are you? I got back from Tokyo yesterday, and I have to fly to Berlin tomorrow. I wanted to squeeze a quick visit in to the poor, wounded soldier and see how you're doing, but I've rung your doorbell three times and you haven't answered, and it's so cold on this doorstep. What temperature does it have to be for there to be a risk of hypothermia? Don't answer that. I can Google it. Why didn't you answer the door? Oh my God, have you had a fall? Do you need me to call for an ambulance? What 's the number? Stupid question. It's 999, isn't it? I knew that. I can do that. How are they going to get in? Maybe I should call the fire brigade too. They can send round some big, brawny men to break the door down. I'll supervise them closely, make sure they don't damage anything except the door."

"Mia, slow down." Was it my imagination or had Ferris relaxed slightly when I'd said her name? Who had he thought it was? "No need for an ambulance. I haven't had a fall. I'm not ninety-two." Ferris chuckled at that one, the bastard. He made an effort to straighten his face once I aimed a pointed glare in his direction, but it wasn't wholly successful.

"Then why aren't you answering the door, sweetie? Are you scared of social contact? Has all this time on your own with only your own broken body to think about made you forget how to interact with people?"

It was so ludicrous that I laughed. "I think that would take years, not weeks." I covered the phone with my hand, looking expectantly at Ferris. "I would very much appreciate it if you could get the door for me. My friend, Mia, is on the doorstep."

"Say please."

"Xan?" She'd screeched it so loud that the sound filtered between my fingers. "There's a dog."

I lifted the phone back to my ear. "One minute."

"It will have eaten me by then."

I sighed, skewering Ferris with a pointed stare. "Please."

Ferris jumped to his feet. "Of course. You only had to ask." He reached out to ruffle my hair as he passed. "Anything for you."

It took all the willpower I had to yank my head away from his touch as if it annoyed me when what I really wanted to do was lean in to it. I pulled the phone back to my ear. "Ferris is coming."

"Who? Oh my God! The dog is looking at me. And it's not on a lead. It has the look of a killer in its eye. Do you think it's got rabies?"

I heard the front door being opened, Mia barreling into the room a minute later in a long, black coat that complemented her ash blonde hair perfectly. She let out a long breath. "That was a close shave."

Ferris appeared behind her with a look of great amusement on his face. "It was a chihuahua."

I bit my lip to stop from laughing. Mia wasn't having any of it, though. "And do you know how aggressive those things can be. Don't be fooled by their size. That's what they want. They want to lull you into a false sense of security and then they go for the jugular. Never mind hellhounds, if Satan would have had any sense, he would have had a bunch of chihuahuas at his disposal."

I ignored Mia and aimed my comment at Ferris. "Mia doesn't like dogs."

Ferris nodded. "I figured."

She turned her attention to him, her gaze sweeping him from head to toe in what was definitely an appreciative glance. "Hello. I'm sorry I didn't introduce myself properly at the door, but I was more interested in sanctuary from the furry beast than making polite chit chat."

I stood and grabbed my crutches. "Ferris, this is Mia. Mia, this is Ferris. We'll go in the kitchen, Mia."

Mia's face crumpled into an expression of great concern. "Oh, look at you, you poor thing. You're very good with those things. If it was me, I would probably just lie on my back like a stranded turtle and demand to be fed grapes."

Ferris shook his head, but luckily Mia had already turned away. He stood back as I led her to the kitchen. She deposited herself in a heap at the kitchen table, pulling the bright pink reindeer toward her and hugging it to her chest. "Do you have any biscuits? I need sugar for the shock."

I shook my head. "I don't think so."

A shout came down the hallway. "There's some chocolate digestives in the top right cupboard."

"Thanks." I closed the door on my way to the cupboard. If Ferris had heard that, that meant he'd be able to hear everything else we said. And I had a feeling I knew what the main topic of conversation was going to be once Mia recovered from the threat of chihuahua attack. I leaned on my crutch to pull the cupboard open. Sure enough, there was a half-eaten packet of chocolate digestives inside, which seeing as I hadn't known it was there, and it hadn't been there before, meant Ferris had been secretly eating them. I was going to be having words with him about keeping biscuits to himself.

There were some things I could put up: a slavish dedication to making me hurt every single day, refusing to do something simple like opening the door without me saying please. But hiding biscuits... that was nothing short of criminal. Although, I suppose he had given up their whereabouts without the threat of torture.

Mia stayed unusually quiet as I set about making two cups of tea and tipped half of the biscuits onto a plate—none of it that straightforward on crutches. Only once I'd delivered my offering—an even more difficult feat—did she tip her head to one side and study me. "Well?"

I frowned. "Well, what?"

She leaned forward, startling slightly as she seemed to realize for the first time that she had hold of a reindeer. Her brow furrowed slightly, but she deposited it on the floor with nothing more than a slight shake of her head. "I come round to see you, expecting to see you at death's door, and instead I find you being waited on hand and foot by the most divine man."

It was unfortunate that I'd just taken a sip of tea. Mia very nearly ended up wearing it. "Oh, I assure you, he does not wait on me hand and foot. Not even close. Why do you think no one answered the door? I just about had to grovel to get him to do it." It was a slight exaggeration, but she didn't need to know that.

"Darling, *who* is he?"

Ah, right. I hadn't actually told her that. I let out a noisy breath. "Miles thought it would be a good idea to hire a live-in nurse. He didn't actually bother to tell me that fact, but that's Miles for you."

Her eyebrows shot up. "He's a nurse."

I smirked. "Allegedly. I have yet to see actual proof beyond an almost masochistic desire to twist me into a pretzel every day."

"Oh really."

I gave her a reproachful look. "Not like that."

"Is he gay?"

"Yes."

She waggled her eyebrows. "Two young gay men stuck in a house together. Whatever do you find to do to fill the time?"

"Not that. I think you've been watching too much porn."

She slid a biscuit off the plate and bit off almost half of it, making a face like she was having an orgasm as she chewed on it. Would Ferris make that same face while eating them? I reprimanded myself immediately. I did not need to be thinking about what he looked like while he was having an orgasm. I was already battling with the overwhelming desire to kiss him.

"Why not?"

"Why not what?"

Mia curled her hands around the mug. "Why haven't you made a move on him? You like him. Any idiot can see that."

I winced. She'd spent all of a minute with the two of us in one room together. If it was that obvious, then I was in real trouble. Shit! Did that mean Ferris knew as well? "That would be a dreadful cliché, surely?"

She gave a dismissive wave of her hand. "Who the fuck cares if it's a cliché. Life is for living. You should try everything once." She held up a finger. "Except for skiing maybe. Look where that got you."

Except if I hadn't gone skiing, I would never have met Ferris, so it was getting more and more difficult to regret my headlong tumble down a mountain.

Mia looked thoughtful. "Is Harvey the problem? Is that it?"

"Harvey?"

"Where is he?" She looked around the kitchen as if she was expecting him to pop out of a cupboard. "Why is he okay with you being shacked up with a hot nurse?"

"He... doesn't know about it." Would it bother him? I hadn't even thought about it. It would have been so easy to take a quick photo of Ferris and send it to Harvey with a message along the lines of 'I've found someone to look after me.' Ferris probably would have posed for it if I'd asked nicely. But that had never been my style, and to be honest—and the realization came as somewhat of a surprise—I didn't care enough. Harvey had waltzed out of my life without so much as a moment's hesitation, and there'd been zero contact since. He had absolutely no right to complain if I'd moved on. *Had I moved on?*

I lifted my head to find Mia staring at me. "Is there a fly in it?"

I blinked at her. "What?"

"In your tea. You were staring at it for so long that I assumed there must have been something in it."

I dropped my gaze to my mug, the surface of the tea free from any insects. "I was thinking."

She picked up another biscuit. "About?"

"Harvey." I paused. "Ferris."

She stopped mid-bite. "Ooh, like a threesome."

I was so stunned for a moment by the direction her mind had traveled in that I was struck dumb. "No. Not like a threesome. Get your mind out of the gutter for once." A sudden image of Harvey cozying up to Ferris came to mind. It made my fingers curl into my palms and my jaw clench. Was Harvey Ferris's type? I couldn't see it. Not when Ferris wasn't impressed by money or status, and Harvey was all about both of those things.

I could however imagine Harvey being interested in Ferris, given that he was hot and had a pulse. The thought of the two of them together made me sweat, and not in a good way. Christ! There was no mistaking the feeling for anything other than what it was. It was pure old-fashioned jealousy. Jealousy that I had absolutely no right to feel. Nothing had happened between me and Ferris, so he could be with whoever he wanted to be with. It wasn't like I could lock him in a dungeon. Mainly because I didn't have one. Oh, and the small matter of kidnapping being a crime.

"He likes you too."

I wrenched my gaze from my tea to stare at Mia. "Ferris?"

She rolled her eyes. "Duh! I'm not talking about Harvey, am I? I'd assume he likes you too given the rollercoaster that your"—she let go of her mug to make finger quotes in the air"—relationship has been on over the last few years. Watching you two was better than any soap opera."

"We weren't that bad." Even I recognized the defensive tone in my voice.

Mia's incredulous stare went on for quite some time. "How many times did you suspect him of cheating on you?"

I dropped my gaze to my tea again. "A few. I never had proof."

She lifted her mug and peered at me over the top of it. "You never looked that hard because you were too scared you might actually find it, and then you would have had to make the break once and for all."

Was there any truth in that? I'd always questioned Harvey on my suspicions, but I'd never asked the other party, or interrogated anyone else who'd been at the same social function and might have known what was going on. "What does that say about me?"

"Which answer do you want?"

I frowned. "What do you mean?"

"Well…" Mia trailed a finger around the rim of her mug. "There's the politically correct one that would be far safer for me to say in case you two aren't really done and this is just another one of your dramas before you fall back into bed, or…"

I prompted her when she went quiet. "Or?"

She grimaced. "Or there's the truth."

"Which is?"

"Are you sure you want it?"

"Yes! You can't just sit there and be all cryptic and then not say what's on your mind."

A hint of a smile appeared on Mia's lips. "Oh, I assure you, darling, I could. I do it all the time at work. 'Yes, that dress looks positively delightful on you. No, the color doesn't make you look like a long dead corpse, not in the slightest. Yes, those photos of you were the best yet. I thought they looked divine. I was so jealous.'"

"Mia?"

She let out a sigh. "You never looked into Harvey's infidelity, of which I suspect there were many, because you just weren't bothered enough." She reached across the table and grabbed hold of my hand. "I'm your friend. If I'd thought for one minute that your feelings for Harvey were about anything more than convenience and sex, I would have spoken up. But he was never going to break your heart because your heart wasn't involved. And if you had ever stumbled across definite proof that he'd been unfaithful, you would have had to end things for good… because you're many things, but you're not a doormat, sweetheart."

I rubbed my fingers over my chin while I considered what she'd said. There was a definite ring of truth to it. "Doesn't that make me a bit of a dick?"

She shrugged. "Or just human. We all have our things that we're in denial about." She slid another biscuit off the plate. "Like the fact that I will convince myself when I am staring at the weighing scales and wondering how on earth I've put on weight, that it couldn't possibly be these biscuits because I only had the one."

"You've had…"

She held up a hand, her glare venomous. "Don't. I let you wallow in your delusions for long enough. At least have the decency to offer me the same courtesy." She took a dainty bite of the biscuit, chewing slowly. "I'm going to make this one last."

I needed to get back to the important thing she'd said. "Why did you say he likes me? Did he say something when he opened the door?"

She fluttered her eyelashes at me innocently. "Who, darling?"

I narrowed my eyes at her.

"Oh, you mean your hot live-in nurse. Did he say anything? He said..." She grinned as if she was recalling something amusing. "He said quite a lot actually in a very short amount of time. He told me that it wasn't too late to pretend that I'd accidentally gone to the wrong address and I wasn't on the doorstep after all. That he was fully prepared to cover for me and pretend it had been an overenthusiastic carol singer, who'd mysteriously lost their voice at the crucial moment due to nerves. He asked if I was prepared to be an observer in the World Grumpiness Championships, of which you were sure to win the gold medal. And he told me that he had ear plugs if I needed them, a tried and tested tactic that was always successful unless you raised your voice, but if you did that he would just move to another room because it took you at least five minutes to get there."

I rubbed a hand through my hair. "Oh yeah, positively brimming with good things to say about me. I can see why you'd get the impression that he likes me."

"Well... you were all he could talk about. And..." She let the silence drag out until I couldn't take it anymore.

"And what?"

"There's the small matter of all the sexual tension brewing between the two of you."

"Is there?"

She nodded slowly. "And it's not all one way. Trust me, I know these things. The real question is what you're going to do about it?"

"He doesn't like models. He dated one once, and he said it's a mistake he's not going to repeat."

"He used those exact words?"

I thought back. "Well, not those exact words, no. But that was the basic gist. And it was like day two of our acquaintance." It seemed so long ago, when in reality it had only been a couple of weeks. I guess living together meant you found out a lot about a person in a very short time.

Mia sat back in her seat and crossed her arms over her chest. "Just kiss him. See what he does. What's the worst that could happen?"

She made it sound so easy. "He could reject me."

Mia let out a very unladylike snort. "Or he might kiss you back and be ever so grateful that you made the first move. You'll never know unless you try, will you?"

I guessed that was true, but the idea was both exciting and scary at the same time, filling me full of a nervous trepidation. What would Ferris do if I tried to kiss him? Mia was right. There was only one way to find out. I needed to take the bull by the horns, or more precisely I needed to take Ferris by the lips.

CHAPTER FOURTEEN

Ferris

December 16th

Xander wasn't an early riser. I was never sure whether it was a side effect of the painkillers he still took at night, or simply the way he'd always been. Whatever it was, I rarely saw him before ten. Given that I was usually up before the larks, it gave me plenty of time to get up to mischief. Today's drive-Xander-crazy-with-Christmas endeavor was to add ceiling decorations. Therefore, while he snored away upstairs, I intended to be busy. Did he snore? I paused to contemplate it. If he did, it was quiet enough not to filter farther than his bedroom. And he'd never done it any of the times he'd fallen asleep on the sofa.

Determined to stop thinking about what Xander might or might not get up to in bed, I made a start in the living room. I stood on a chair to affix the colorful streamers across the length and breadth of the ceiling. Where they crossed each other, I added some long, dangling decorations, which caught the light as they swayed. Perfect. I could already envisage Xander's struggle to pretend he hadn't seen them. He'd lasted less than half an hour with the reindeer, so it would be interesting to see how long he held out with these.

I added tinsel to any possible surface I could, winding it around handles and draping it along bookshelf shelves. Running out of space in the living room, I moved to the hallway and hung the remaining ceiling decorations there. Tiptoeing lightly up the stairs and avoiding the one that always creaks, I lingered outside Xander's bedroom for a moment. Definitely no snoring. Starting at the top, I wound gold tinsel around the entire length of the banister until I'd reached the bottom.

It was still only nine, so I quickly added a nativity scene to the living room. I'd had to improvise a bit, the shop out of stock of the more traditional constituents that usually made up a nativity scene. It didn't matter. It looked even better if you asked me. More modern. Tradition was okay, but individual flair trumped it every time. Who wanted something that looked exactly like what everyone else had? Xander probably. But tough luck. He was still in bed, so he didn't get a say.

I'd made a start on breakfast by the time the usual creaking emanated from above. I went and stood in the hallway, Xander and his crutches appearing at the top of the stairs a moment later. "Morning, sunshine."

He lifted his head to skewer me with a look that said he was not only not awake yet, but he was barely in the land of the living. He lowered his hand to the banister but paused before it made contact. "What's...? No, never mind. If I ask that question, you'll tell me it's tinsel, and you'll probably also tell me who invented it and for what reason."

I gave him my brightest smile. "Germany, sometime in the 17th century. I want to say 1610, but I have to admit that I'd have to doublecheck that fact. It was originally made out of shredded silver, and it was used to decorate sculptures rather than Christmas trees."

From the expression on Xander's face, you would have thought I'd just told him that cow dung made an excellent face pack. He shook his head. "How do you know that stuff? I'm also not going to ask why it's on my banister because you'll just tell me it's Christmas, like it's perfectly normal to cover every spare inch of your home in something sparkly that will have to come down in a few weeks. What a waste of time and effort."

Xander scratched his abdomen, his T-shirt riding up to reveal tanned bare skin, his sweatpants hanging particularly low. I swallowed the sudden onrush of saliva that flooded my mouth.

"Don't you think?"

"Huh!" I forced my gaze to Xander's face. "Don't I think what?"

"That it's a waste of time and effort."

"But it's *my* time and effort, not yours. And... it's worth it to put that sunny smile on your face."

Xander poked at the piece of tinsel in a way that suggested he wasn't entirely sure that it wasn't harboring some sort of tiny creature, maybe a Christmas elf that would take up residence in the skirting boards if he didn't keep an eye on it. I cast a quick eye back to the kitchen to check there was no smoke coming from the grill. "Are you going to stand up there all day?"

"Possibly."

"Fine. *I'll* eat your breakfast, then." I turned on my heel to head back to the kitchen. "Don't go in the living room."

I could hear him grumbling all the way down the stairs as I turned the bacon and sausages over. I grinned as he bypassed the kitchen and headed straight to the living room. He was nothing but predictable. He appeared in the kitchen a couple of minutes later, easing himself into his usual seat at the kitchen table. I poured a cup of coffee and pushed it over to him. "It looks great, right?"

He took a large swallow. "It looks like my living room has turned into Santa's Grotto. I wouldn't have been surprised to find a large bearded man in the corner asking if I wanted to sit on his lap for a special treat."

I bit my lip to keep myself from smiling as I placed a plate full of food in front of him. "You might want to keep those sorts of fantasies to yourself."

"You know exactly what I meant."

I turned to get my own plate and took the seat opposite. "Are you calling him Daddy when you sit on his lap?"

Xander pointed his knife at me. "You're not funny."

"What three words *would* you use to describe me?" I was genuinely interested in what he might come up with.

Xander's gaze slid away from mine, the kitchen cabinet apparently holding great fascination for him. He'd done that the previous night as well, ever since Mia's visit. It made me wonder what the two of them could possibly have talked about to make him suddenly so self-conscious. He shrugged. "I don't know."

"Try. And then I'll do you."

He heaved out a dramatic sigh that said I was forcing him to recite one of the works of Shakespeare by memory rather than simply coming up with three adjectives. How hard could three words be? "First one that comes into your head."

"Biscuit hoarder."

"That's two words, and it's not true."

Xander's gaze finally returned to mine, the look in his eyes distinctly accusatory. "Did I know about the biscuits?"

"I didn't know you needed to know about the biscuits. Do you need to know about everything I've bought since I've been here?" I pointed at the cupboard under the sink. "There's drain cleaner in there in case you need to know about that." I thought hard before clicking my fingers. "The bulb in the bathroom needed replacing. I bought one of those as well. In fact, they only came in packs of two, so there's a spare one in the bathroom cupboard." I took a bite of the breakfast I'd almost forgotten about. "Three words."

Xander's brow scrunched. "I just gave one."

"That one has been disqualified from consideration."

"By who."

"The council of bad decisions and outright lies."

He laughed. "And let me guess, the council is you?"

"President, chairman and founding member."

"More like the council of bullshit."

"That's next door. We have joint meetings once a month to make sure we keep our stories straight."

Xander took a sip of his coffee. "Nurse."

"You're dreadful at this."

"You are a nurse."

I stared him down. "You might as well just say man. I'm that as well but it would be a really boring and obvious thing to say." I took pity on him. "I'll do you first, then."

I tapped out a tune on the table. *Sexy!* I couldn't say that without getting myself into a whole heap of trouble. *Gorgeous.* Also, not a good idea. "Insufferable."

Xander's jaw firmed as he lifted his hand to point. "You know where the door is."

"I do. I go in and out of it when I bring food so that you don't starve to death. You probably thought it appeared magically in your cupboards."

"Not magically, but it's probably hidden—like the biscuits."

I got up from the table to grab the offending items from the cupboard. Sitting back down, I pushed them across the table toward him. "There you go, you can shut up about the biscuits now. Think of it as an early Christmas present."

Xander tipped his head to one side. "So for Christmas you've got me a half-eaten packet of biscuits? You really shouldn't have. Your generosity knows no bounds. I wonder what I'll get on the actual day. A Muiller Crunch Corner where you've already eaten the chocolate bits and I just get the yoghurt, maybe? Some chewing gum that you've already chewed? A gobstopper down to its last layer?"

I nodded slowly. "All very good ideas. I need to write these down. Where's a pen when you need one?"

Xander just grunted.

I smiled. "Pessimist."

He frowned. "What?"

"That's my second word for you."

"I'm not!"

"I notice you didn't argue about being called insufferable."

He cut off a piece of sausage angrily. "I've thought of another for you."

"Go on."

"Wind-up merchant."

I made a tsk tsk sound. "Three words. Use your fingers if you need to count. Do you want to know your last word?"

"Not particularly. I'm not sure my ego can take it on top of being an insufferable pessimist."

I stifled a smirk. "I tell you what, I'll give you a choice of three." I thought about it carefully. "Entertaining. Amusing. Likeable."

Xander paused mid-chew, his plate almost empty. "You couldn't give me those as the three."

"Nope. Your ego would have grown to gargantuan proportions. You have enough problems with getting around without struggling to get your head through the door."

Xander wiped his mouth and sat back. "I'll take… likeable. Okay, here's yours."

I braced myself. I'd given it out so the very least I could do was take it with good humor.

"Manipulative."

Not too bad. I knew a few other people who would have thrown that my way as well.

"Evil."

Ouch. That was a bit harsh.

Xander waved his knife at me again. "And that's because you take great delight in making me do those damn exercises."

"The exercises that are helping you to get better, but go on." Xander was slower to come up with the third. "Give me a choice of three."

He rolled his eyes. "I love the way the rules keep changing."

"Blame the council."

He drummed his fingers on the table. Would he follow the same pattern I had and actually go for something nice for the third one or would he go for the full put-down? "Enthusiastic, intelligent, or unique—that's your choice."

I didn't even have to think about it. "I'll take unique every time."

Xander's gaze skittered away again. "You're definitely unique."

From the way he'd said it, I wasn't entirely he'd meant it as a compliment.

·♥·♥·♥·♥·♥·

One thing I'd noticed about Xander cutting down on the painkillers was that when he did take them, they seemed to have a much greater effect on him. He was obviously sensitive to their effects anyway, but limit them to once a day and that seemed to multiply. Therefore, it didn't come as too great a surprise when I entered the living room to find him laid on the floor.

I went and stood over him. "You doing extra exercises?"

He rolled over onto his back. "You have a one-track mind."

If I did, it certainly wasn't about exercises, not with Xander blinking up at me with bedroom eyes and an expression that I could imagine him wearing after sex. It made me want to lower myself gently on top of him and… I wasn't going to take that thought any further. "That's me. I eat, breathe and sleep physio. I should have become a physiotherapist really."

"You should have become a…" A deep furrow appeared on Xander's brow. He rolled his head to the side as if he was searching for inspiration, his gaze alighting on the nativity scene I'd set up. "Not a Christmas decorator, that's for sure."

I lowered myself so I was sat cross-legged next to him, my fingers a hairs breadth from his arm. "That's not a job."

"Not for you, it isn't."

Xander reached across and picked up the Captain America model. "Who's he meant to represent?"

"Well, he's stood by the manger, so take your pick from Mary and Joseph."

Xander's fingers moved across to the opposite side of the manger where Iron Man stood. "No way Tony Stark is going to be Mary, so he'll have to be Joseph." He finger-walked over to the other three figures. "Who are these?"

I tutted. "You really have to ask, the three wise men." Except I'd had to use Star Wars figurines as a perfectly good substitute.

Xander looked thoughtful, or as thoughtful as you could look when codeine was turning all your synapses to slush. "Wouldn't Princess Leia have been better as Mary?"

"Sexist!"

He made an adorable little sound that I think was meant to be a snort, but he didn't quite manage to pull off. "What gifts are they going to give? Lightsabers, spaceships, and wookiees."

"All incredibly useful things. Jesus would have benefitted greatly from any of those things. Far more than I'm sure he did from frankincense and myrrh."

"Oh, you're not dissing the gold, then?"

"Who could ever say that gold is not useful? You're wrong about the third one, though. No way Han Solo is giving Chewie away. He'd probably give a laser gun, or just a pithy one liner. This is Jesus, the son of God, and what would Han say…? I know."

Xander wasn't listening. He'd started up a one-man rerun of the nativity story, complete with all the dialogue and sound effects. It would have put any primary school to shame. He'd got as far as the shepherds, for which I didn't have any figurines, but the Star Wars lot were apparently versatile enough to play more than one part, when his eyelids started to drift closed.

I let my fingers do what they'd been itching to do ever since I'd sat down. I let them bridge the gap and curl around Xander's arm to give him a gentle shake, the skin warm and supple beneath my fingertips. "Hey, sleepyhead. You can't sleep here."

Xander didn't open his eyes. "Can. S'comfortable. New carpet. Expensive."

"It won't be comfortable when you've slept here. Your pelvis won't thank you for it." I gave his arm a tug, but he barely stirred. I really should have ushered him off to bed before now, but it had been strangely peaceful to spend time with him, even if he was drugged up to the eyeballs. And then there was the fact that he'd been so entertaining.

Xander's eyelashes fluttered. "Need a new one."

I chuckled. "A new pelvis?"

"Yeah!"

"You don't even know what you're talking about, do you?"

"Wookiees."

"Well, that definitely proves my point."

I let go of his arm and stood, readjusting my position so that I was astride him, a position which made it far easier to peel him off the floor. He didn't resist, but he didn't exactly help either. His eyes were still closed by the time I had him leaned against me, his head coming to rest on my shoulder. "Are we dancing?"

I slid my arm around his waist to give him extra stability. "I don't think you're up for it tonight. But if you're offering, I'll definitely hold you to it some other time."

"Don't dance."

"Shame." It was a shame. I could definitely spend more time with Xander Cole pressed against me, one part of my body enjoying it far more than the rest. It was perhaps as well that I doubted Xander would remember any of this the following day. It was for that reason that I let the moment linger, wrapping my arms more tightly around him and savoring it.

Xander turned his head, his lips pressing against my neck. "Are you going to take me to bed?"

My cock twitched, and I had to have stern words with it about Xander not meaning it the way I wanted to interpret it. The fact one of his hands had slipped to curl around my ass didn't exactly help the situation either. Apparently a drugged-up Xander was a touchy feely one. "I am." My voice came out decidedly husky, and I had to clear my throat. "Think you can use your crutches?"

"Sick of crutches."

"I know. But you won't be on them much longer." And then it wouldn't just be the crutches he wouldn't need anymore, it would be me as well, the realization sending a spear of emotion into my chest. I'd gotten used to having Xander in my life. There would definitely be a Xander shaped hole once this arrangement came to an end. Could we be friends? Would he want to be friends? Or would he just drift back to his old life and forget I existed. "You're so adorable." The words slipped out before I could stop them.

I went still, but if Xander had heard me he didn't react. There was no way he was getting up the stairs under his own steam, which left me with two choices. I either needed to put him to bed on the sofa or carry him upstairs. Knowing he would have a far better night's sleep in his own bed, I chose the latter. I lowered him into a seated position on the sofa, using it as a midway point to maneuver him over my shoulder into the best parody of a fireman's carry I could manage. Xander was heavy enough that it took me a while to get him up the stairs. But eventually we made it and I was able to roll him beneath the covers. "Do I undress you?"

Xander didn't answer, his breathing that of someone already asleep. I decided against it. I needed to sleep, not replay the memory of unwrapping Xander like the best Christmas present a man could ever ask for. I pulled the covers up to his chin and spent a moment watching him asleep. Yeah, definitely adorable. I dropped a quick kiss on his forehead and then got out of there before I could do something stupid like curl up next to him.

CHAPTER FIFTEEN

Xander

December 17th

I hardly dared go downstairs. Every day had a new manifestation of Christmas popping up in my house. First, it had been the tree, then the reindeer, and then the ceiling decorations. And of course, you couldn't forget the nativity scene. That's if you could call it that. What did you do when you couldn't source the correct religious figures? Well, if you were Ferris, you apparently performed a holy union between Captain America and Iron Man, and had Han Solo, Luke Skywalker and Princess Leia bringing the gifts. As for the animals in the manger, they consisted of an eclectic mix more likely to be found on the savannas of Africa, the giraffe looking particularly pleased to have been invited to the birth of Christ.

Ferris was nowhere to be seen as I reached the bottom of the stairs. That in itself was suspicious. I cocked my head to the side, listening, but was met with silence. I started in the living room, an examination revealing nothing more sinister than the same decorations that had greeted me previously. I made my way to the kitchen, apologizing to the zebra as I inadvertently knocked him over with the end of my crutch. There was nothing in the kitchen either. In fact, I couldn't find anything that hadn't already been there the day before. Had Ferris run out of ideas? I found that hard to believe.

The front door opened, Ferris stepping inside and stamping snow off his boots, a plastic bag of shopping hanging from each hand.

I narrowed my eyes at him. "What did you do?"

He lifted his head, a huge smile crossing his face when he saw me standing there. "You're up early. I went shopping. If I hadn't, your breakfast would have been an empty plate."

"Before that?"

He frowned. "Brushed my teeth. Got dressed. The supermarket tends to frown on nudity. They really need to get with the times. Although, it is December, so I probably would have gone with clothes anyway."

"Christmas related."

"Ah!" Awareness sparked in his eyes, the smile transforming into a smirk. "I thought the game we were playing is that you pretend not to notice my little festive touches?"

"I noticed. I can't see my ceiling anymore, and my living room has been taken over by tiny zoo animals and giant reindeer. So, the fact that there is nothing for me to pretend I haven't noticed is extremely concerning. It makes me worry you're going to give me glitter for breakfast."

Ferris grinned. "Now there's an idea. How do you like it, grilled or fried?"

I didn't deign to answer, trailing after him as he carried the bags into the kitchen and started unpacking what he'd bought. I flung open one of the kitchen cupboards, but there was nothing there that I wouldn't expect to see.

"What did you think I'd put in there?"

I shrugged, and Ferris smiled. "Maybe I didn't add anything."

I regarded him silently. "I don't believe that for one minute."

Ferris placed another couple of items into a cupboard. "Okay, then maybe you're not looking in the right place."

"I've looked everywhere."

"Uh-huh!"

I did a quick inventory, retracing my steps mentally and conceding that my words were true. I'd been everywhere in the house. *In* the house. "Fuck!"

I retraced my steps to the living room window. Even before I reached it, I could tell that something was wrong. It might be December, and therefore gloomy, but it normally let at least a bit of light in. It couldn't now though, not with the huge inflatable snowman bobbing about in front of it.

Ferris appeared at my shoulder. "Too much?"

I couldn't help it. I started laughing. "My life used to be so simple before I met you."

"Boring, right?"

"Something like that."

We both watched it for a moment, its movement growing more violent as the wind picked up. Ferris turned his head my way. "If it helps, it was a lot bigger than I thought it was going to be."

"I bet you say to that to all the boys."

Ferris's shoulder tensed against mine. It wasn't like him not to have an immediate comeback. He was usually the king of flirting, so what had changed? Whatever it was I didn't like it. I nudged him with my shoulder. "Oh, come on, you've got to have an answer for that one."

He let out a soft laugh. "Not this time."

I turned my attention back to the sight outside my window. "So where did the giant snowman come from?"

"A friend."

"It's funny, you seem to have a lot of friends with oversized Christmas ornaments to hand. Is that your criteria for making friends?"

"Definitely. They have to fill out a questionnaire detailing all their worldly possessions before they can make it onto my shortlist."

"My neighbors are going to complain."

"About my rules for making friends."

"About the huge monstrosity outside my window."

Ferris screwed his face up. "You're injured. They wouldn't dare."

I shook my head. "I've got to ask, was there any point after seeing how big it was that you reconsidered your decision to plonk it in my garden?"

"Nope. I didn't want to disappoint you."

The urge to kiss him was back. Actually, if I was honest, it had never gone away, Mia's words making it ten times more difficult to bury the urge and pretend it didn't exist. "I don't think you could ever disappoint me. But... you should probably stop now."

Amusement glinted in his eyes. "Thank fuck for that. I was running out of ideas. All I had left was sneaking into your bedroom and covering you in tinsel."

"Lucky for me that there's a lock on the door, then, isn't it?"

Ferris's gaze strayed across the room to his abstract nativity scene. "What do you remember about last night?"

"Last night?" I frowned. "I took a couple of painkillers and then went to bed. I obviously zonked out straightaway because I didn't even bother to get undressed. What am I supposed to be remembering? Did I say something stupid?"

Ferris shook his head.

Was it my imagination or did he look relieved?

· ♥ · ♥ · ♥ · ♥ · ♥ ·

Ferris pulled a table in front of the sofa, depositing a glass of water, along with the two painkillers that helped me to sleep. I groaned as he added a third item—a pack of cards. "Do we have to?"

He lowered himself into a cross-legged position on the other side of the table, picking up the deck, and giving them the sort of shuffle a croupier would have been proud of. "You love playing cards with me."

"You cheat."

"I do not!"

I swallowed first one pill, and then the other. "How do you explain the ace that just happened to drop out of your sleeve the other day, then? Going to tell me that it'd been there since you got dressed in the morning?"

Ferris winked. "It was a strange coincidence indeed. Especially seeing as it was the exact card I needed. Fate was definitely smiling on me that day. I tell you what I'll do." He placed the cards down, pulling his T-shirt over his head and dropping it on the floor next to him. "There you go. Now no more cards can accidentally get stuck anywhere. Happy?"

I was, but not for the reason he was referring to. Ever since that first day where he'd treated me to a view of him in a towel, he'd remained frustratingly clothed, my subconscious lamenting the fact that I hadn't taken a better look when I'd had the chance. I leaned forward, using the excuse of spotting the tattoo on his shoulder to touch. "What's this?"

He turned his shoulder so that I could see it properly, my fingers brushing his skin as he moved. The tattoo was of a cross with a loop at the top. "It's an ankh." When I looked at him blankly, he elaborated. "It's the Egyptian hieroglyphic for life. It's meant to bring good luck."

"Does it work?"

He laughed. "I keep waiting for it to kick in. I reckon it must be soon."

For the next thirty minutes, I was thoroughly trounced at gin rummy. Ferris put it down to the fact that he'd had to teach me to play and I was still trying to get my head around the game. But I suspected it was more to do with the fact that my interest lay more in the man playing the game than the game itself. Ferris was larger than life in everything he did, and playing cards was no exception. He kept up a constant stream of anecdotes while he played, most of them washing over me. I was far more interested in watching him, noting the dark sweep of his eyelashes as he laughed, and the way he talked with his hands, not letting the fact that one was full of cards hold him back. Every now and again when he smiled, which was often, there would be a teasing glimpse of dimples to enjoy as well. I had it bad, and the urge to do something about it was getting stronger by the minute. What was the worst that could happen?

Ferris's hands were a blur as he dealt the cards. "You'll win this one. I can feel it. I can't have all the luck."

I leaned forward, unable to resist any longer, sealing my lips over his. Ferris froze, his body turning to stone and his lips not softening in the way I'd hoped. Even though it wasn't the reaction I'd been after, I hung in there, hope springing eternal that it was just because I'd surprised him. He'd relax and the kiss would happen. It had to. I couldn't conceive of any other result, not when I wanted it so damn much. Fingers planted themselves on my chest, the push gentle, but still nevertheless a push, a clear message in it encouraging me to stop.

Ferris's smile was tight, his gaze fixed on something over my right shoulder. "Those painkillers are pretty strong, hey?"

I stared at him, struggling to process what he meant. "You think I only kissed you because of the painkillers?" It didn't help that my words were slightly slurred.

"I think…" He shook his head, as if changing his mind about what he'd been going to say. "They definitely make you go slightly loopy." He inclined his head toward the nativity scene. "You reenacted the whole Christmas story last night, complete with noises for all the animals. And when you didn't know what noise an antelope made, you just made it up. While I'll admit to not knowing it myself, I highly doubt it's a cross between a wolf and a monkey. And you don't even remember that, do you?"

So that's why he'd asked earlier that day what I remembered. I stared at the nativity scene, trying to conjure up the memory, but it remained frustratingly out of reach. I stopped trying. It was hardly the most important thing at the moment. "I didn't try to kiss you because of the painkillers. I've wanted to kiss you for a while." There, I'd said it. I sat back. The rejection had hit me far more than I was prepared to let on. He'd been the one doing all the damn flirting. Almost the first words out of his mouth had been a come-on, telling me that he could give one hell of a ride. "I hope you're not expecting me to apologize for kissing you?"

"No, of course not. Listen…" Ferris paused, as if he was running what he'd been about to say through his head first. Given the usual verbal diarrhea that spewed from him, that was hurtful too. "It's not a good idea, is it?"

I took the positives I could from what he'd said, focusing on the fact that he hadn't said he wasn't interested in me or that I was barking up the wrong tree. "Why not?"

"Reasons."

"Give me three." I held three fingers up in the air to illustrate my point.

His brow furrowed. "Why three? Isn't one enough?"

"Humor me. And what you said about the painkillers doesn't count." I quickly lowered the extra finger I was holding up, the one that had decided it wanted to keep the other three company.

He propped his chin on his hand, looking thoughtful. "You have a boyfriend—"

"Ex-boyfriend."

Ferris raised an eyebrow. "You didn't seem too sure of that to start with."

"I am sure." How could I not be? I hadn't had so much as a text from Harvey for weeks. He was probably reveling in his newfound single status and making sure anything with a pulse was aware of it.

"We're from very different worlds, you and I."

I let my lip curl. "That's such a fucking cliché. Modeling is my job. It's not who I am. So I have to travel every now and again. I always come back. This is my home."

Ferris went silent. I held up two fingers, carefully counting to make sure there were only two. "That's two reasons. What's the third?"

The wait for him to answer stretched on interminably. Finally, he shook his head, the ghost of a smile hovering on his lips. "I've got nothing."

At least he hadn't dredged up his unwillingness to date models again. That would have been an easy third option to go for. I took my time leaning forward, giving him plenty of time to move back should he wish. He didn't. He stayed right where he was. It only took a second to close the space between us until our lips touched again. My heart leapt as this time he responded. It was the sweetest kiss I'd ever experienced, so sweet that I couldn't stop myself from smiling as I continued to kiss him. The awkward position of leaning forward left my pelvis throbbing, but I didn't care. Ferris was worth a bit of pain.

When the kiss finally came to an end, I let my fingers trail over his cheek, unwilling to go from so much contact to none in the blink of an eye.

He smiled back at me. "I didn't think that was going to happen."

"No?"

He shook his head. "But I'm glad it did."

"Me too."

I turned my head, taking in the assembled audience of African animals who'd watched us getting it on. "They look pleased as well."

Ferris laughed. "You should go to bed before the painkillers really kick in, or we'll have a rerun of last night where I had to carry you."

"You carried me to bed?"

He nodded.

"But you didn't undress me." It was a statement rather than a question. Obviously, he hadn't because I'd still been wearing sweatpants when I woke up.

"I felt like that would be taking rather too many liberties. Besides, call me picky, but I prefer my men conscious."

"That is picky." I heaved myself to my feet, Ferris standing as well. His close proximity meant it was inevitable that I took the opportunity to steal another kiss. The second was just as sweet as the first had been. The urge to invite him to my room was almost overwhelming, but I could already feel the drug-induced stupor trying to drag me down. I knew from experience that I'd be asleep as soon as my head touched the pillow. Therefore, it wasn't the time for making any promises I wouldn't be able to keep. Besides, I didn't need to rush things. He'd still be there tomorrow. Just as annoying and just as tempting.

CHAPTER SIXTEEN

Xander

December 18th

"What?"

The fact I was smiling like an idiot to the point where Ferris needed to call me on it might have been embarrassing if it wasn't for the fact that he kept doing it too. "Just happy."

He nearly choked on his coffee. "You? Happy? Jesus! Should I check the painkillers, make sure you haven't taken an accidental overdose?"

"Not necessary." I leaned forward over the table. "I haven't taken any this morning. I didn't want to be accused of only making a move because I was under the influence of opioids."

Ferris's lips quirked. "Now, who would be stupid enough to say a thing like that?"

I shrugged. "No idea."

He shuffled forward, meeting me halfway. "So… what has brought on this sudden bout of happiness?"

He was fishing. We both knew it, but I was only too happy to tell him what he wanted to hear. Well, almost. "Your lips."

Ferris pulled back an inch. "Oh, just my lips, is it? I'm more than just a pair of lips, you know?"

I let my gaze travel slowly down over his chest, pretending to appraise him. It was so freeing not to have to hide it any more. "I can see that. You have arms and legs and a nose, and a—"

It was his turn to shut me up by kissing me, which had been my plan all along. I slid my fingers into his hair, slanting our mouths together at the perfect angle to tease and taste. He tasted of coffee. We probably both did. The kiss was everything

I remembered from the previous night and more. And this time there could be no mistaking that I was under the influence of drugs. We were both smiling when we separated.

Ferris sat back and winked, the next words out of his mouth wiping the smile off my face instantaneously. "Exercise time."

I shook my head. "That's not what you're supposed to say. You're supposed to suggest that we spend the day kissing, and that the exercises can wait for one day."

He crossed his arms over his chest. "You're a good kisser, Xander Cole, but you're not that good. Exercises first. Kissing later."

Now that was an offer I could get on board with. "Deal."

December 20th

I pulled Ferris closer, wanting to taste, wanting to plunder his mouth and keep plundering it until it belonged to no one except me. I was lying on the sofa, Ferris half sprawled across my body, but careful to keep the majority of his weight off me. We were still clothed, but that didn't stop our hands from wandering freely. I'd lost track of how long we'd been kissing. It didn't matter. It wasn't like either of us had anywhere we needed to be. I slid my hand into his hair, altering the angle slightly to deepen the kiss. He writhed against me, pushing an unmistakable hardness against my thigh that matched my own growing erection. We hadn't planned on getting hot and heavy; it had just happened.

A familiar noise broke through the haze of lust, the ringtone telling me that I needed to answer it. I reluctantly pulled my lips from Ferris's, his little murmur of protest making it that much more difficult. "It's Miles. If I don't answer it, he'll freak out and send the fire brigade round."

I dropped one more kiss on Ferris's lips before reaching for my phone. Ferris made no move to climb off the sofa, curling up next to me, his fingers tracing the curve of my jaw. "Hey, Miles."

"I thought you were never going to answer. What were you doing?"

Thoroughly kissing a gorgeous nurse, and I resent the hell out of you for interrupting that. "My phone wasn't next to me. You know I can't move that fast."

"Yeah, sorry."

The genuine contrition in my brother's voice made me feel guilty for lying, but I had no intention of spilling my secrets over the phone. Ferris and I were shiny and new, and I wanted to keep things just between the two of us for as long as I could. There would be plenty of time after Christmas to admit to falling for the man I hadn't even wanted in the house initially. Miles might have met Ferris, but that didn't mean he wouldn't get any ridiculous notions in his head about predatory nurses jumping on me when I was too weak to fight them off, when nothing could be further from the truth. "How are the kids?"

Miles started to relay stories about what they'd gotten up to, his voice taking on its usual edge whenever Clarissa was mentioned. Theirs was a relationship of tolerance for the sake of the kids, still tinged with occasional bitterness. It made me glad to be gay. I jumped as Ferris's fingers strayed to my crotch, tracing the outline of my hard cock beneath the fabric. He raised an eyebrow in question, but when I didn't protest continued his soft exploration while I tried to work out what I'd missed Miles saying while my attention had been elsewhere.

"...anyway, it was fun, even with the crazed squirrel. How are you doing? Is Ferris looking after you?"

I dipped my head just in time to see Ferris's fingers disappear beneath the waistband of my sweatpants. We'd kept it to kissing only for the last couple of days, with some heavy petting over clothes, so this was new. And I had absolutely zero objections. Due to a lack of underwear, I only had to wait a few seconds before warm fingers fastened around my cock. I stifled a groan, managing to turn it into a cough. "Oh yeah, he's looking after me. Like you wouldn't believe actually."

Ferris muffled his snort in the curve of my neck, his hand starting a slow stroke over my cock that reminded me just how long it had been since I'd last had an orgasm. I was probably going to last about 3.2 seconds, which made getting rid of my brother an urgent priority. I really didn't want to come with his voice in my ear. That was all sorts of wrong.

Miles made a noise of approval. "That's good to hear, and I'm so glad that you eventually came around to the idea of having a nurse."

I had, but my version of 'having a nurse' and Miles's were very different. "Well, yeah, you know I can be stubborn. Listen Miles, I've got to go. I've got to..." *Get my hands on Ferris's cock, and come. Not necessarily in that order.* "... make some phone calls. Work stuff."

"This close to Christmas?"

"I know, it sucks. I'll see you on the 27th, right?"

"Yeah the 27th. My flight should be—"

I hung up before he'd finished his sentence. If he questioned it later, I'd blame the weather or something for a faulty line. I let out the groan that had been fighting to get free for the last few minutes. "You're a very naughty boy, Ferris... Shit! I feel like when you have me three seconds from orgasm I should at the very least know your last name."

His hand stilled. "Night. As in the bit after day, rather than the type that hang around castles. And if you're three seconds from orgasm, I better slow down a bit."

I reached for him, Ferris helping in the quest to free his own cock from the confines of his jeans. Even so, it seemed like a frustratingly long time before I was able to wrap my hand around it. His cock was perfect. Just like him. I captured his lips again, my tongue sliding against his as the two of us managed to settle into a mutually beneficial rhythm. Without lube, we settled for spit. There was no way I was stopping to give directions to Ferris so he could find it in my room, and if I went myself the mood would be well and truly gone by the time I got there and back on my crutches. Besides, what we were doing was just fine. More than fine. Lips strayed from mine, skimming along the length of my jaw to whisper husky words directly in my ear. "Are you alright? Tell me if you're in pain and I'll stop."

"Don't you dare stop, not when I'm so close."

That seemed to spur Ferris on, my orgasm hitting within a minute, Ferris continuing to stroke my sensitized flesh through the aftershocks coursing through my body. He followed soon after, his gasp of pleasure as his cock pulsed in my hand one of the most beautiful sounds I'd ever heard. We both lay back, the room filling with the sound of our ragged breathing. I held my hand up in front of me, Ferris laughing at the sticky evidence of his orgasm. He levered himself off me, climbing over me with great care. "Wait there. I'll get a towel."

He was gone less than a minute, returning with a towel as promised and putting it to good use in soaking up as many traces of cum as he could find. There was no fixing the spots that had already soaked into my sweatpants, and I didn't even want to think about the sofa. What we both needed was a shower, but I wasn't about to complain as he dropped the towel on the floor before tucking himself back into my side, his fingers tracing circular patterns over my chest. "Sorry, we probably should have discussed that first. You know, rather than me attacking you when you were on the phone."

I turned my head to see him better, noting the genuine concern in his eyes. "I would have stopped you if I hadn't wanted it. *Never* apologize for giving me a hand job!"

He grinned, letting his head *thunk* back on my chest. "It was good though."

"It *was* good."

He was quiet for a few moments, alarm bells starting to ring in my mind. Was he regretting taking it that far? I'd thought that we were both on the same page, but could I have got it wrong?

Ferris craned his neck back to look at me. "What are you doing for Christmas?"

Huh! That's what he'd been thinking about. "What do you mean?"

He plucked my hand off his thigh, interlocking our fingers together and staring at them as if they required all his concentration. "I mean, Christmas Day. Miles isn't back till the 27th, so…"

I was pretty sure I knew where he was going with this, but I didn't want to jump to conclusions and risk looking like an overeager buffoon. "You know what I'm doing, sitting around being a grumpy bastard, probably still doing my physio exercises because my nurse is such a slave driver that I'll never hear the end of it if I don't, even though it would just be for one day. The lecture just isn't worth it."

I got a smile for that comment, Ferris still giving far too much focus to our hands. "Only… we could… spend it together, if you wanted?"

It took all the willpower I had not to turn into the Cheshire Cat. Not that Ferris would have noticed. Apart from a quick glance, he was still refusing to look my way.

"What about your mum?"

He pulled a face. "You think I want to go and spend it with her and Mr. Sleaze? I'm sure she'd prefer it to be just be the two of them." He finally met my eyes. "Crap! That came out wrong. That's not why I suggested it. I asked because I'd prefer to spend the day with you, but I'll understand if you want some time on your own."

"Would you? Are you sure you wouldn't just keep jumping up and down in front of the window?"

Ferris's lips twitched. "Sounds a bit energetic. I might pitch a tent in the garden though, which by the way, is not a euphemism."

I laughed, risking pain to turn sideways on the sofa to face him. "I'd love to spend Christmas with you."

He tapped me on the nose with his finger, a move meant to distract me from the huge grin decorating his face, one that rivaled mine from earlier. "While you're being so amenable, want to come to a party with me?"

I frowned. "A party. What, like a Christmas party?"

"New Year's Eve actually. It's at St Thomas's, the hospital where I used to work. Well, not actually at the hospital. We don't conga around the hospital beds. Not anymore, not since we got into trouble for it. The party is at the Walrus Bar just over the road."

"If you don't work there anymore, how come you're still going to the party?"

Ferris stared at me incredulously. "Please tell me, Xander, that that's not a genuine question. The poor people are already deprived of getting to work with me in the future. I can't possibly deprive them of my presence at a party as well. There'll be riots. There'll be petitions. There'll be…"

I borrowed one of his favorite gestures, rolling my eyes at him. "Alright Mr. Popular, I get the drift. Your fans need you there or their evening just won't be complete. I appreciate the invitation, but I doubt I'll be up for partying by then."

Ferris obviously wasn't giving up that easily. "You'd get to dance with me."

I nearly choked on my own tongue. "Why in the world would you think that would convince me? I don't dance. Ask anyone."

He quirked an eyebrow. "You tried to dance with me the other night."

I lifted my head to stare at him. "I did not. When?"

Ferris smirked. "The same night you put on the one-man nativity show." He dropped his voice to a husky whisper. "Please dance with me, Ferris. I want to feel your body pressed against mine. I want to know what it feels like to be in your arms. Please make my dreams come true."

I burst out laughing. "Yeah, right. They were painkillers, not LSD."

He sighed. "Alright, you don't have to dance, but say you'll come."

I shook my head. "You don't need to be looking after an invalid all night. You'll have a much better time on your own."

Ferris nodded, but I could see the disappointment in his eyes. "It's probably not your scene anyway. No A-list stars and a distinct lack of champagne." I let the comment go. Ferris would eventually realize that the hole he kept trying to force me into just because I had a career in modeling didn't really fit.

CHAPTER SEVENTEEN

Ferris

December 20th

Things were good. In fact, things were better than good between Xander and myself. It really hadn't seemed like a big deal to add sex to the domestic routine that we'd already had going on. And it certainly gave us something else to do during the day, one mutual hand job turning into many more.

The man in question was currently laid on the sofa, squinting at a crossword that I knew full well he'd never be able to finish. He usually got about halfway and then gave up, pretending that he was bored. I sat forward and stared at him. "Do you remember what you said when you kissed me that first time, about having wanted to kiss me for a while?"

Xander gave a grunt without lifting his eyes from the newspaper.

"How long?"

"How long what?"

He knew exactly what I was asking. "When did you first want to kiss me? It was when you opened the door to me on that first day, wasn't it?"

Narrowed green eyes pinned me in place. "That's a joke, right? Did you think I was calling the police to ask them to lock me up before the overwhelming lust I felt for you blazed out of control?"

"It's quite possible."

Xander snorted. "All I wanted was you off my doorstep."

"So when?"

He put the newspaper down. "I don't know."

"Try and remember."

He sighed. "Definitely when you dragged me out in the snow. I remember that. But probably before then."

"In the snow!" I chuckled. "Oh, you old romantic, you." I easily ducked the cushion that came winging toward me. It took Captain America, Iron Man and the manger out in one fell swoop. "Look what you've done. I'm sure it's blasphemous to throw a cushion at Jesus."

"I wasn't throwing it at Jesus. You should have protected him. Therefore, the fault lies with you."

I retrieved the figures and arranged them neatly again. "You were weird with me after the chat with your friend."

"Mia?"

I nodded.

Xander sat up straight. "That's because she used all her woman's intuition to announce that you liked me too, and she told me to go for it."

"You couldn't tell from the way I was flirting with you?" It was a genuine question.

Xander shrugged, looking decidedly sheepish. "You might have been like that with everyone."

I thought about it. "I'm not. Only the chosen few."

"Good to know." Something gleamed in Xander's eye. "What about you?"

"What about me?"

He stretched, deliberately letting the T-shirt he was wearing ride up so that I got an eyeful of toned abdomen. "At what point did you realize you were desperate to get your hands on me?"

I screwed my face up. "Erm… desperate. Not sure that's the word I'd use. I mean… your brother showed me a nice photo, so that was good advertising and was definitely an incentive for taking the job, that and all the groveling he did to '*please* take his brother off his hands.' But then I was met at the door by an angry, sweaty wreck dressed in a bathrobe, who looked like he'd just been run over by a truck. You're lucky I didn't ask if Xander Cole knew he had squatters. Perhaps it was me that should have called the police. So yeah, definitely not then."

Xander picked the newspaper back up and threw a disparaging glance at the crossword. "I'm bored of this now."

I disguised my smirk as a cough. "Let's go out."

Xander's brow scrunched up. "Out?"

"I want to take you on a date."

"A date?"

"Are you just going to repeat everything I say? Could be fun. Try this one. Ferris Night is the sexiest man in the universe. I am so lucky to get to share the same air as him. He is the moon to my stars, the yin to my yang. He is—"

"A date, where?"

I thought about it. I'd said it completely on impulse, but now it was out there I wanted nothing more than to make it happen. I might have kissed and caressed Xander Cole, but I hadn't been out on a date with him. Unless you counted the Natural History Museum. In which case I'd made Dorothy a third wheel, so I was very much inclined not to count that. "I want to take you out to dinner."

Xander quirked a brow. "So you don't have to cook?"

"No! Although, that does make it an even more attractive proposition. What do you say?"

"How?" Xander jerked his chin toward his crutches. And I'm not going out for a date in a wheelchair, so don't even suggest that."

"I wasn't going to. I gave the wheelchair back, remember. We call a cab. Crutches to cab. Cab parks outside restaurant. Crutches to restaurant. You sit and eat. Simple."

Xander didn't look too convinced. I understood his reticence. The need for crutches did turn the simplest thing into a bit of a performance. "Do you want to go out for dinner with me or not?"

His lips curved into a slow smile. "Yes."

The definite answer along with the lack of hesitation had something fluttering in my gut. It was the sweetest "yes" I'd ever heard. I jumped to my feet, my enthusiasm for the idea growing by the second. "Then I suggest we get ready." I checked my watch. "What do you say I meet you in the kitchen in an hour. Is that enough time for you to make yourself look pretty for me?"

"Pretty?"

I bounded across the space and dropped a quick kiss on his forehead. If I kissed anything else, we wouldn't end up going anywhere. "Prettier."

Xander let out a huff. "You called me a wreck."

I bit my lip to keep from laughing. "You were that day." I let my gaze trail slowly down the length of his body. "Now... you're not." I pulled him gently to his feet. "Get ready."

·♥·♥·♥·♥·♥·

I was the first to arrive in the kitchen. It was stupid that I was nervous when it was just Xander, but I was. It was like I'd taken the little bubble we'd been existing in and had turned it into something more official. What were we anyway? Were we boyfriends? Or was I getting way ahead of myself? Could we work in the real world? Or was this just a Christmas fling? It didn't feel like a fling. Not on my part anyway. Unfortunately, I wasn't privy to what lay inside Xander's brain.

When Xander finally appeared, he was a sight to behold. I'd gotten used to him in sweatpants and a T-shirt, and it wasn't like he wasn't attractive even in those clothes, but dressed in black jeans, a cream jumper and a dark jacket, he was positively scrumptious. He'd shaved and styled his hair as well, and there was a delicious scent of some expensive aftershave wafting from him. The whole package left me tongue-tied and seeking to recover my equilibrium while I stared at him.

I gave myself a mental shake and called his name. "Xander!" His brow scrunched at the way I'd shouted it despite being less than a few meters away from him. "Hey, Xander. Come quick. Someone's broken into your house. They're smoking hot, though, so I vote we tie them up and keep them. And you'll never believe who they look like. They look a lot like that model, Xander Cole. You know the one, he has that faraway look in his eyes in his photographs that drives everyone crazy trying to work out who or what he's thinking about."

Xander rolled his eyes and shook his head as he maneuvered himself across the kitchen on his crutches until he was standing right in front of me. "You're an idiot. And in answer to your question, I'm usually thinking about how much longer it's going to take because I assure you that it's a long way from the glamorous world it's made out to be. It's hard work, you know." He grimaced. "And I've just said that to a nurse, which makes me a condescending dick. Sorry. In a whose job is harder competition, I'm sure you'd win hands down. At least I get a big pay cheque at the end of it for doing very little. Yeah, I'm a bad person. I deserve…"

A flustered Xander Cole digging himself into a big hole was an even more adorable one. "A spanking?"

Xander snorted. "Something like that. Not before dinner, though." He gave me a quick once over, the gleam in his eye as his gaze ran over my jeans, shirt, and leather jacket ensemble telling me that I most definitely passed muster. "You look like you did when you first arrived."

"I was trying to make a good impression."

"And there I was thinking you were a salesman." He grinned. "I've changed my mind. Whatever it is you're selling, I'll have some."

"Just myself." I frowned. "That came out wrong. I'm not offering myself as some sort of rent boy."

Xander's lips quirked. "Shame. That would have been quite some investment."

"Well, *you*"—I wrapped my fingers around the back of his neck and pulled him in for a quick kiss—"can have it for free."

Xander's lips curved against mine. "In that case, I am a very lucky boy."

"You are. And I intend to remind you of that fact at least twice a day. Three times on a Sunday." Yeah, it definitely didn't feel like a fling. It felt like the start of something. My phone vibrated and I pulled it out of my pocket to see that the cab was outside.

·♥·♥·♥·♥·♥·

Snow covered pavements weren't ideal for crutches, so we took our time getting from the curb to the Italian restaurant, Xander looking distinctly relieved once we'd been seated and left to peruse the menu. I'd picked a fairly small intimate place, our seats tucked away in a corner close to the ornate Christmas tree.

Xander lifted his head from the menu with a thoughtful expression on his face, the candlelight lending his features an attractive glow. "Who's paying for this meal?"

I leaned forward. "You know what I…" About to say love, I quickly changed it. "…like about you. It's that romantic streak you have. Here we are… beautiful ambience… candlelight… soft music playing in the background." Given it was Christmas music, and our seats were right next to the tree, I'd almost expected Xander to balk at it and demand a table in the kitchen. "And what do you want to talk about? Not feelings. Not how wonderful it is to get to go on a date with me. None of those things. No, you want to talk about money."

Xander raised an eyebrow. "Me, then."

I tipped my head to the side. "We should compare our pay cheques and see who earns more. The winner pays for dinner."

Xander's eye roll was tinged with amusement. "So, like I said, *me* then."

I grinned unashamedly at him. "I'm joking. I asked you out on a date. What sort of man would I be to do that and then let you pay?"

"A broke one who claimed that if I didn't put a roof over his head, he would be forced to seek out a soup kitchen and take up residence on the streets."

I held my thumb and forefinger up with barely half an inch of space between them. "I may have exaggerated a tiny bit. I'm paying."

Xander shook his head. "No, listen, I'll pay. I don't mind."

I coughed loudly. "You might not mind, but I do. I'll never hear the end of it. You'll throw it back in my face every opportunity you get."

Xander clasped a hand to his chest in mock horror. "Me? If I don't pay, you'll hold it against me forever. It's just not worth it. I'm paying."

I shook my head. "No, you're not."

Xander crossed his arms over his chest. "I am."

"Over my dead body."

"That can be arranged."

I snorted. "Really? You and whose army? You're not exactly hard to run away from. I can be at the end of the street before you've even got hold of your crutches."

Xander pasted his best affronted expression on his face. "I don't think nurses should mock their patients."

"You're not my patient. Not officially anyway. You are officially a pain in the arse, though. This was my idea, so I'm paying. End of discussion."

Xander's eyes narrowed to slits. "Says who? Who made you king of deciding when discussions come to an end?"

A quiet cough at the side of the table had us both turning our heads to find a dark-haired waitress stood there holding an iPad, her expression one of distinct amusement. "Sorry to interrupt, gentleman, but most people wait until they've at least ordered something before they start arguing about who's going to pay."

It was a good point. Technically, there wasn't anything to pay for yet. I pulled the menu more firmly in front of me. "Is that so? Well, we're very forward thinking. Always looking to the future, that's us."

The waitress chuckled. "How long have you been married?"

I watched in amusement as Xander started to choke on nothing but air. "Oh, a long time. And I've got to tell you that marriage just never gets any easier." I dropped my gaze to her right hand. "I can see you've still got that to look forward to." I leaned forward in a conspiratorial fashion, inviting her to meet me halfway. She didn't hesitate, looking to me in a way which said she expected me to impart great wisdom. Well, I'd do my best. "The secret is to never take things to heart too much."

Xander finally remembered how to breathe again—and talk. "We're not married."

I shook my head sadly, maintaining eye contact with the waitress and ignoring Xander completely. "See. When he says things like that, it really wounds. It's like a knife to the chest. It desecrates all those years of beautiful memories, the ceremony, the celebrity guests we had, the pigeons we released after saying our vows. We couldn't get hold of doves at short notice, so we had to improvise." I gave a dramatic shrug. "But what can you do? You just have to take it on the chin and tell yourself that he doesn't really mean it, that his denial comes from a good place, and that we can get through it, that—"

"Ferris!" There was a world of warning in the way Xander said my name. A warning that said if I didn't stop, I was probably going to end up eating dinner on my own.

I sat back in my chair, holding my hands up in defeat as I met his narrowed stare. "Okay, we're not married. This is our first date."

The waitress's gaze zig-zagged back and forth between us, as if she wasn't quite sure which version of events to believe. "Oh!" Her brow furrowed, and she was silent for the longest time. Finally, she took a step back. "I tell you what, I'm going to give you a little longer to decide what you want to eat." Her retreat from the table could only have been described as hasty.

Xander propped his chin on his hand. "Pigeons?"

I sighed. "Alright, fine. We'll have doves like everyone else. I didn't know you were such a traditionalist."

"Except we're not getting married."

I winked. "I agree that it would be a little fast to go from first date to marriage all in one night. What are you doing next week?"

Xander blinked a few times and then dropped his gaze to the menu. "I need wine."

"It won't mix well with the painkillers."

He met my gaze, a strange intensity in his expression. "I figured I wouldn't take any tonight. I thought it might be nice for you to have a conscious date past ten o'clock."

"That would be… nice." I let my hand stray across the table until our fingers were almost touching. "Although… you are much quieter and more amenable when you're unconscious. And what are you going to do with this night of lucidity?" I asked the question, despite the fact that I could already see the answer burning in Xander's eyes. It made heat rise in my chest, my jeans suddenly becoming far too snug.

Xander smiled. It was a seductive smile I'd seen grace numerous magazine covers during my extensive research on the internet. Only this time, it wasn't aimed at an unseeing audience. It was aimed at me. And it packed quite a punch. "You'll have to wait and see."

Shit! I looked around for the waitress. I'd really wanted to come on this date. But now we were here, all I wanted to do was find out what would happen after it, and whether Xander really was going to live up to the promise in his eyes.

·♥·♥·♥·♥·♥·

Xander leaned back against his bedroom door. Everything we'd done so far had been confined to the sofa, so it felt like a huge step. Either that or I was reading far too much into what accounted to a change of scenery. "Are you sure about this?"

Xander frowned. "It's just a bedroom."

I nodded slowly. "It is a bedroom. A very un-Christmassy bedroom, but a bedroom nonetheless."

"Want me to fill the bed with reindeer?"

My lips twitched. "That is such a sweet offer, but I think I'd be concerned that you'd only have eyes for them. I couldn't bear playing third wheel to an inanimate object that wasn't even a sex toy."

"I could wrap tinsel around my—"

I kissed him, gently but inexorably, keenly aware of Xander's lack of balance. "It's pretty enough. It doesn't need any decoration." Reaching around him, I opened the door. "Get in."

Xander arched an eyebrow. "Wow. Bossy. I'm not about to unleash a monster, am I?"

I waggled my eyebrows and deliberately dropped my gaze to the already swelling bulge in my jeans. "Depends on your viewpoint, I suppose."

We both laughed. Xander discarded his crutches and sat on the edge of the bed. I let the door close and came to stand in front of him, resting my hands gently on his shoulders. He lifted his hand, his fingers brushing the front of my jeans and gently tracing the line of my zipper. Desperate to be released, my cock twitched, the next words out of my mouth completely at odds with what I actually wanted. "We don't have to do anything."

Xander looked up at me from beneath his lashes, just the merest sliver of green on show. "I don't even know if I can. But I want to."

"What do you want?" We'd never discussed what Xander preferred in bed, whether he was a dedicated top or bottom, or whether he was versatile. As someone who was versatile myself, it didn't matter one way or the other. However, it did make a difference to what was going to be possible given the constraints of Xander's pelvic injury.

A slight flush appeared on Xander's cheeks. "I want you to fuck me."

"That's definitely possible."

"Yeah?"

Xander sounded surprised and I smiled, sliding my hands inward so I could trace the warm skin of his neck with my thumbs. "I don't know what you normally do for sex, but there are positions that don't involve swinging from the lampshade."

"I don't want it to be boring."

"Boring?" I stared at him for a moment, bursting out laughing when I saw he was serious. "Xander, you could never be boring, in or out of bed." I traced his jawline, anticipation bringing me out in goosebumps. "Take your clothes off. All of them."

Xander's hands moved to the hem of his T-shirt. He'd already left his jacket in the living room downstairs. "What about you?"

I shrugged my jacket off my shoulders and let it fall to the floor. "Right there with you."

I only got a slight glimpse of his smile before it disappeared behind a layer of fabric. It was worth it when I was rewarded with a naked torso moments later. I drank him in, the glimpses I'd seen when his clothes had ridden up, or from the V of his bathrobe, not doing him justice. I ached to touch, to show him tribute with both hands and mouth. I intended to take absolutely everything that was on offer tonight. Xander lifted a foot off the ground. "Can you take my shoes off?"

I stared at him open-mouthed. "Seriously? Nurse, cook, butler, and now I'm a valet as well. What next? Want me to accompany you on your next modeling shoot? Perhaps I can hold things for the photographer. Unless it's…" I didn't finish that thought. Xander's ex had absolutely no place in this room, so I wasn't going to say his name. He was an idiot who'd been stupid enough to abandon Xander when he'd needed him the most. He'd made his choice and his loss was my gain. It felt like if I said his name, he'd appear behind us like some sort of cock-blocking apparition.

Xander chuckled. "It'll be faster if you do it."

"Oh well, if it'll be faster." I yanked one shoe off, his sock coming as well, before repeating the action with the other. "Anything else I can do for you, sir. Need a shirt pressing? Want me to source a new cravat for you? Perhaps you'd like me to have a new suit made up for you at the tailors."

Smiling, Xander dispensed with his trousers as I made fast work of my own clothes. Once we were both down to underwear, I climbed on the bed with him, Xander rearranging himself so that we were facing each other on our sides. I kissed him, each kiss growing progressively deeper and longer, Xander rolling into me like it was exactly where he belonged, my thigh wedged between his. My cock throbbed with need as I trailed my fingers down the length of his spine until they had nowhere else to go but to dip beneath his underwear. His skin was heated. Or perhaps it was mine. It was difficult to tell when we were plastered together.

I pulled back slightly so I could see Xander's face. He'd always been stunning, but with his pupils dilated and his desire there plain to see, he was even more beautiful.

I couldn't remember ever wanting someone as much as I wanted Xander. It was almost scary in its intensity. I'd come here for a short-term job that would provide me with a place to stay, and I'd found so much more than that. Life could be so strange sometimes. Who could ever have thought that a tumble down a ski slope and a flooded apartment could have led to a moment like this?

A furrow appeared on Xander's brow. "What's brought on that look?"

"What look?"

He smiled. "It's not so much deer caught in headlights as confused rabbit not even sure what the big, bright lights are and where they've come from."

"I don't know." I did know, but I wasn't ready to share my thoughts with him quite yet. Not until I knew we were both on the same page. "I was just thinking."

"Oh, well that's really flattering, thank you. You stick your hand down my pants and then you start thinking about something else. Perhaps you'd like a book to read. Or I could put the TV on."

I rolled him gently onto his back and divested him of his underwear, his cock hard and swollen against his abdomen. "Not necessary. I've found something interesting to look at."

"I hope you're going to do more than look."

I gave him a mock glare. "You're so impatient."

"Ferris!"

I smiled as I pressed a kiss to his hipbone, before turning my attention to the livid scar where fencepost and thigh had become intimately acquainted.

Xander lifted his head to see what I was looking at. "I told you my underwear modeling days are over."

I pressed a kiss to the scar. "Good."

He frowned. "Why is that good?"

I considered a lie but, in the end, went for the truth. "I don't want anyone else seeing you in your underwear?" It sounded even more possessive than it had in my head, but it was too late to take it back.

"Oh!"

To stop Xander from dwelling on it for too long, I slid my lips over his cock. As distraction tactics went, it worked like a dream, nothing but incoherent grunts and moans spilling from his lips as I worked him with lips, tongue, and throat, his fingers clutching at my hair as I showed him every trick I knew, and some that I'd invented just for him.

I didn't stop until the taste of precum had grown strong enough that I knew if I carried on, he was going to come. He tapped my hip to urge me upwards. "Come here."

He didn't have to ask twice. Being careful not to put any weight on him, I shed my boxers and straddled him, the head of my cock in line with his lips. His fingers curved around my ass cheeks to urge me forward. From there, it was easy to slide between Xander's lips and into my own personal nirvana. I closed my eyes and gave in to sensation as Xander treated me to a skilled blow job that had my balls drawing up tight in no time at all. I wanted to come in his mouth, but not today. Today, I wanted to give him what he'd asked for.

Mustering some willpower, I pulled out. "Have you got condoms?" If he said, no, I wasn't sure what I'd do. I hadn't packed any because it had never crossed my mind that there was a possibility of anything sexual creeping into my dealings with Xander Cole. And even in the last week, as our relationship had developed, I hadn't wanted to be guilty of jumping to conclusions. There was a shop a few streets away. Did they sell condoms? Would Xander still be awake by the time I got back?

"Nightstand. There's lube as well."

I scrambled over there so quickly that I nearly pitched headfirst off the bed in my haste, Xander's laughter filling the silence. "Don't laugh. If I fracture my pelvis, it'll be months before we can do this."

Xander reached over to trail his fingers down my back. "I don't think I can wait that long."

I knew how he felt. I wasn't sure I could wait a few minutes, never mind months. I found the condoms and lube, relief flooding through me as I freed one from the foil packet and rolled it over my cock. I added plenty of lube before turning back to Xander. He eyed my cock hungrily before lifting his gaze to mine. "You better have this all worked out or I swear I'm going to kill you. And I'll have zero regrets about it."

I rolled him over onto his side, encouraging him to bend his knees. "I've never had threats during sex before. I imagine this must be what it's like for the poor male praying mantis. I have a newfound appreciation for their plight." I slid in behind Xander and tucked my body into his. "How does that feel? Is it comfortable? Any pain? And be honest, because we really don't have to do this today." I didn't add that now we were this close to it, that I'd probably cry if we didn't. Especially now that I had the curve of Xander's extremely tantalizing ass presented to me in such an alluring fashion. I needed to be inside him more than I needed to breathe.

Xander shifted slightly, as if he was trying the position out. "It's fine."

"Good." I slid lubed fingers between the cleft of his ass until I reached my target. "But you have to promise to let me know if you're in any pain and I'll stop. We can suck each other off instead."

Xander's grunt sounded like it was the last thing he wanted to do. That made two of us. "I promise."

The words were somewhat grudging but it was the best I was going to get. I pushed the tip of a lubed finger inside him, waiting until he relaxed before going deeper. Once he could take it, I introduced two. I wanted him good and ready.

I kissed his shoulder and neck as I finger fucked him, Xander starting to writhe on my fingers as I rubbed them over his prostate.

"Fuck me, Ferris."

I laughed against his neck, my fingers keeping up that same rhythm deep inside him. "What was that? I couldn't hear you."

"Ferris!"

My name was more of a keening whine on his lips than an actual word. I liked the sound of it. A few more rubs of his prostate and I withdrew my fingers. A part of me would have loved to have seen him come from nothing more than the stimulation of my fingers inside him, but my cock wasn't remotely on board with that idea. I trailed my lips along the warm skin of his neck, tasting the tangy salt of his skin. "Are you ready?"

"I hope you don't actually expect an answer to that."

"I'll take that as a yes." I shifted so that the tip of my cock was lined up with where it needed to be, anticipation simmering beneath my skin. "Don't move. Let me do all the work."

Xander's chest shook as he laughed. "I was intending to."

I pushed forward, Xander loose enough from me having worked him with my fingers that I sank straight in. It was a toss-up which sound was loudest, my exclamation of "Jesus," or his gasp. Sliding my arm around him, I flattened my palm against his chest. It was mainly to hold him in place so that he didn't get too lively and hurt himself in the process, but it did come with the added bonus of being able to trace the contours of his chest with my fingers while I fucked him.

With the need to be gentle playing on a constant loop in my brain, I made an experimental thrust. It was only a small movement, but even so the delicious friction had a tingle of electricity arcing down my spine and settling in my balls. "Does this work?"

"It works."

Xander's reply was breathless and tinged with desperation. His back was an inferno against my chest as I gradually increased the pace, sliding deep into his tight ass. Unable to reach his mouth, I had to settle for kissing his neck, but it was a small price to pay for the fact we were actually doing this. Xander's breathing was ragged, but then I could hardly talk, not when my own was escaping in pants in time to each thrust of my hips.

How the hell had I taken a job and ended up with *this*? And it wasn't just sex. I might be balls deep in Xander's ass, but the maelstrom of emotion coursing through my body was about far more than just physical pleasure. I slid my hand down to Xander's stomach, the muscles trembling beneath my palm. He released a little purr of approval as I wrapped my fingers around his cock, letting the movement of my hips push it into the tight embrace of my hand. *Gentle.* It was becoming increasingly difficult to listen to that reminder in my head, the desire to hammer into Xander growing by the minute.

"Close."

I knew he was. I could feel it in the coiled intensity of his body and in the velvet hardness of his cock in my fist. I stroked him harder and fucked him deeper, managing to coordinate the two movements to give him maximum pleasure. It was like some sort of exquisite torture, the edges of an orgasm starting to curl around my synapses so slowly that I wasn't entirely sure I could come like this.

"Yes. Like that. Yes. God."

And then Xander was coming, his cock pulsing in my hand and his ass clamping down on me. And just like that, a switch was flipped, my orgasm hitting me out of nowhere. I gripped onto him, my fingers digging into his skin as I rode the waves of sensation until they eventually started to subside, leaving me a shaky, sweating mess, my face buried in the curve of Xander's equally sweaty shoulder. "Are you okay?"

There was a long pause. "Define okay."

It took willpower to lift my head so I could peer over his shoulder and search for signs of strain on his face. "Not in pain. Not worried that sexual activity has put you back. Not regretting what we just did."

Xander gave a slow nod. "Oh, in that case I'm absolutely fine."

I took the opportunity to get rid of the condom in the wastepaper bin by the bed. When I turned back, Xander had rolled onto his back and was watching me from beneath his eyelashes. The sight of the pearly droplets of fluid that had escaped from the firm grip of my hand mixing with the sweat on his abdomen was momentarily distracting, my cock twitching like it wanted to go again. "What?"

He smirked. "Mind getting the ketchup for me?"

I stared at him. "The ketchup?"

"Yeah, I have to eat you now, right?"

I lay down next to him, turning my head his way. "If you eat me, we can never do that again."

Xander let out a pained sigh. "That's a good point."

"And you have to take all the Christmas decorations down yourself."

"An even better point." He turned his head toward me, his smile making something leap in my chest. "Alright, we'll postpone the eating. Until after Christmas."

I leaned forward and stole the kiss that I'd been craving during sex, Xander leaning into it like he'd missed it too. My phone beeped on the nightstand, Xander pulling a face. "Who's that?"

I reached across and tilted the screen so I could read the message.

Maggie: *Sorry to contact you so late, Ferris, but Simon is concerned you didn't get the message a couple of days ago that your apartment was ready to move into. Please contact me asap and we can organize a time for you to pick up the keys. I'm sure you're eager to get everything sorted before Christmas.*

Eager wasn't the word I'd use. Why would I be eager to leave Xander and move into a place where there was no banter, no sex, no laughing? Things were just fine the way they were. Would Xander expect me to leave if I told him? Or would he ask me to stay? I wasn't sure I was ready to test that out. Not yet.

"Something wrong?"

I dropped my phone back on the nightstand. "Nope. It's nothing important." I turned back to Xander and shuffled closer until our noses were almost touching. "Where were we?"

CHAPTER EIGHTEEN

Ferris

December 23rd

I was upstairs when the doorbell rang just before midday. Xander's friend, Mia maybe? She'd said that if there were no problems with flights she'd try and pop in again before Christmas. No doubt she wanted to find out whether Xander had taken her advice and made a move on me. I guessed I owed her a huge debt of gratitude for that one. Who knows how long the two of us might have danced round each other if she hadn't given him a metaphorical shove in the right direction? Yeah, if it was her, she could eat all of the biscuits that I'd bought yesterday and Xander didn't know about. I raised my voice so that my voice could be heard downstairs. "Do you want me to get it?"

Xander's shout came back from the living room. "No! I wouldn't want you to strain yourself."

I grinned as I finished straightening the duvet on Xander's bed. Although, given the amount of time I'd spent in it in the last few days, it was beginning to feel like mine as well. I'd barely set foot in my own room except to grab clothes. There hadn't been any need to, Xander making it perfectly clear that I was welcome in his bed. even if all we did was sleep. I still hadn't found a way of casually dropping my new flat being ready into conversation, and I was beginning to think it was better to wait until after Christmas. Xander's brother would be back on the 27th anyway. Once he was, Xander and I could talk and work out what the future held for us.

I was halfway down the stairs when Xander pulled the front door open. Not Mia. Not the postman. Not carol singers. Not even a salesman. I recognized the man immediately from the photos on the internet, the one of him and Xander locking lips virtually having burned itself into my retinas. Harvey fucking Walker. Here. On Xander's doorstep. And he looked tanned and impossibly stylish, like he would have been just as much at home in front of the camera as he would operating it.

What was he doing here? Had Xander known he was coming? I dismissed the thought immediately. Xander might be good at many things, but keeping a secret wasn't one of them.

I took the rest of the stairs much slower, a multitude of facts making themselves known. Harvey had a suitcase. Harvey thought he was staying here. Harvey had just leaned forward to drop a lingering kiss on Xander's lips and Xander had done nothing to stop him.

Harvey smiled at Xander. "Hey, babe. It's fucking freezing here. I can't wait to get in and warm up."

Bile rose in my throat as Xander stepped aside and let him past, the front door swinging shut behind him. He was meant to be telling him to get the fuck out. Why wasn't he? It was like watching some sort of soap opera. Only, it was one I had a starring role in.

Harvey paused in the hallway, rolling his shoulders back in a way that said he was easing a crick in his neck. "I've got to say you're looking a lot better than the last time I saw you. I was worried."

He hadn't noticed me on the stairs. Neither had Xander. Abandoning his suitcase in the middle of the hallway, Harvey headed straight for the living room with Xander trailing in his wake.

I'd reached the bottom of the stairs by that time, close enough that I could hear Harvey's exclamation as he entered the living room, the living room that I'd spent a lot of time turning from an emotionless cold space into something far cozier.

"Jesus! Who set a tasteless Christmas bomb off in here?" I reached the door in time to witness Harvey turning in a slow circle, surveying his surroundings as if he was assessing earthquake damage. His lip curled. "Don't worry. I can fix it." He picked up a purple glittery reindeer, eyeing it as if it was one of the most distasteful things he'd ever seen in his life.

Xander finally spoke. "Harvey, what are you doing here?"

At least it confirmed that I'd been right about Xander not expecting him. Although, that was cold comfort when Xander sounded more curious than annoyed at his unexpected arrival. Harvey finally noticed me standing in the doorway, his gaze slowly raking me from head to toe and pausing at my bare feet before making the journey back to my face, nothing more than slight curiosity on his face, as if I was of very little consequence and he just needed me fitting neatly into a box with a label. "Who's this, Xander?"

Xander looked like someone had asked him the quiz question to end all quiz questions, the one that if he got wrong would lead to his execution. It didn't bode well, a huge stone forming in the pit of my stomach. "This is Ferris. He's…" How hard could it be to tell your ex that you'd moved on, that said ex was no longer in the picture? Except Harvey wasn't acting like his ex. Not in the slightest. He was acting like someone who thought he could just stroll in and pick up where they'd left off. "He's a nurse that Miles hired. He was concerned about me being on my own while he was in Spain. Ferris, this is… Harvey."

A nurse! I didn't know whether to laugh or cry. After everything we'd shared, the weeks we'd spent together, laughing, baiting each other, sharing stories, making love. *That's* what I was. Nothing but a nurse. I had a sudden new empathy for how Jesus must have felt when his disciples denied him in the garden of Gethsemane. I stared at Xander, not caring if he could see the hurt in my expression. It did hurt to be reduced to nothing more than a nurse. Except Xander wasn't looking at me. He was looking at Harvey.

I muttered something that hopefully passed for a greeting, Harvey gracing me with a cursory nod and then turning away. He deposited the purple reindeer on the floor, examining his hands in a way that said he was concerned about contamination. "Good old Miles. I was worried about you too, but you know how important the Chanel campaign was. There was no way I could turn it down. And then of course there was the Christmas party at Susan Beringer's house. She'd never have forgiven me if I missed it. I came as soon as I could, though. I've missed you, babe. I can't wait to spend Christmas with you."

I'd heard enough. I slipped out of the door and headed straight for the stairs, and more importantly the sanctity of the spare room, where I'd have the opportunity to collect my thoughts. Once I'd reached it, it was automatic to start packing, my hands needing something to do while I tried to corral the events of the past few minutes into some sort of sense. Harvey Walker had waltzed in like he'd never been gone. It was obvious that for him nothing was amiss, which meant either Xander had lied to me, or Harvey was living in cloud cuckoo land. Which was the truth? I forced myself to breathe, to think about it rationally, my fingers gripping on to the edge of my bag as I considered everything I knew. Could Xander be that manipulative?

I relaxed slightly as all the evidence pointed to the answer being no. Oblivious, yes. Stupid, definitely. But not manipulative, and not a liar. Just because he was a model didn't mean he was anything like Jack, so I needed to be careful not to let my past color the present. But that left me at a crossroads. I could either stick around and put pressure on Xander to make the right decision, to choose me, or I could do the right thing and give him space and time to make his own mind up. What if Harvey was who he truly wanted? I didn't want to be with him, knowing that I was second choice. It was far better to leave with my head held high and see what happened next.

Bag half packed, I grabbed a piece of paper and a pen and scribbled a quick note.

Xander,

I'm going to do the right thing and give you space to sort things out. I hope that things will work out the way I want them to. I can't tell you how much I hope that. But I'm not going to put pressure on you. Do what's right for you. Call me when you ready to speak to me on 07700 900205.

Love Ferris X

I laid it carefully on top of the chest of drawers before returning to packing my bag.

"You're leaving?"

I hadn't even heard Xander come up the stairs. I didn't look his way as I concentrated on stuffing items in the bag without bothering to fold them first. I'd worry about what state they were in later. "I think it's for the best, don't you?"

"You think I lied to you? I didn't, I swear."

I let out a heavy sigh, steeling myself before turning to face him. "I should have listened to my gut about the whole thing. You know, the fact that you never did seem too sure about your relationship status."

"We *did* split up."

I laughed, but even to my own ears there was very little humor in it. "I think you might need to tell the man downstairs that, because with all the calling you babe, and arriving to spend Christmas with you, I'm sensing he doesn't think so."

Guilt flashed across Xander's face. "Where will you go?"

I grimaced. This wasn't how I'd wanted to break the news to Xander, but given everything else that had happened, it suddenly didn't seem important that I hadn't mentioned it. "My new flat's ready. I probably should have told you, but... yeah..." I fastened my bag and put my shoes on, slipping into my leather jacket before slinging the bag over my shoulder. "You're better now, anyway. You should be able to get rid of the crutches in a few days and use a cane instead." I managed to force a smile. "Funny what actually doing physio can achieve."

Xander didn't return my smile. He was silent as he followed me to the top of the stairs.

"Babe?"

The shout had come from the kitchen. I squeezed the banister harder than I needed to, my knuckles going white. "You'd better answer him."

Xander's pause was long before he finally did. "What?"

"You haven't got any soya milk."

"Why would I? I don't drink it."

I took the opportunity while Xander was busy to make my way down the stairs. I'd gotten halfway before Xander called my name.

I kept going, not pausing to look back until I'd reached the bottom of the stairs.

Whatever Xander saw on my face had him grimacing. "Stay. Please. I can sort this. I just need some time."

God, it was tempting. It was also tempting to march into the kitchen and tell Mr. Bigshot Photographer to get the hell out, that his presence was very much not required, that we'd been doing absolutely fine without him there. But getting rid of him wasn't down to me.

I sighed. "I might have done if you'd introduced me as something other than a nurse hired by your brother." I regretted the words as soon as they were out of my mouth. It was a low blow, designed to hurt Xander the way he'd hurt me, and that kind of tit for tat thinking wasn't going to help either of us. I knew why he'd done it. He'd found himself floundering in a situation he hadn't been prepared for. To say anything else at that time would have turned awkward into confrontational. Is that really what I would have wanted? That's exactly why I needed to take myself out of the picture.

I shook my head. "Actually, you know what, that doesn't matter. You were put on the spot, and you did what you thought was right. I might have done the same in your shoes. Sort your shit out, Xander, decide what it is you really want, and then give me a call if that happens to have anything to do with me. Then we can talk."

I turned before I could change my mind, my focus on the front door.

"Wait."

I didn't wait. I was already wavering. All Xander had to do was look at me with those pretty green eyes of his and I would cave spectacularly. Then I'd end up a lurking presence in the background while whatever was going to transpire between Xander and Harvey ran its course, which could be anything from a break-up to a reunion.

Thoughts of the latter sent a shard of pain through my chest as I fumbled the front door open. I set off without any real direction in mind, most of the snow having melted to slush overnight. I couldn't help seeing it as some sort of metaphor for mine and Xander's relationship, as if it was Harvey's footsteps that had turned the white prettiness gray. I walked quickly with the knowledge that should Xander try to follow he would have no chance of keeping up with me. I would be well away before he even made it down the stairs. Only when I was a few streets away did I look around for a bus stop.

Thirty minutes later, I was home. Only it didn't feel like home. My new flat was empty and cold and completely devoid of any hint of Christmas. It wasn't flooded, but that was about the only positive I could come up with. I'd had my stuff delivered there, but none of it was unpacked. I wandered from room to room, nothing but piles of boxes and furniture to greet me. And of course, there was no Xander, the place so silent that it seemed to be mocking me. I gave brief thought to locating the kettle, but I couldn't seem to muster the energy even for that.

I jumped as my phone rang, a smile spreading across my face. It would be Xander telling me that he'd gotten rid of Harvey and begging me to come back. My optimism was quickly dashed at the sight of 'Mum calling' on the screen. Just what I needed.

"Hey Mum." I did my best to inject a bit of levity in my voice.

"Ferris?"

I could tell something wasn't right straight away from the catch in her voice. "Yeah, it's me. What's wrong?"

"You're probably busy."

I stared at the closest pile of boxes, the boxes that I had zero interest in unpacking. "I'm not busy at all."

"It's… Barry."

My fingers tightened around the phone. "What about him?"

"He's…" My mum let out a sob. "I found out that he's been cheating on me. She's a barmaid at the local pub. I don't know how long it's been going on. He says not long, but…"

Fuck! "Really? Shit! I'm so sorry, Mum."

She sniffed. "I wondered if you could come round. I know you're probably busy with Xander, and the last thing you want is to be a shoulder for me to cry on. After all, it's Christmas…" Her next words were indecipherable as she started to cry harder.

"Where is Barry?"

"I threw him out. I threw his clothes in the street as well. It was like something out of *Eastenders*." She gave a strangled laugh. "You would have been proud of me. Only now I'm wondering if I did the right thing."

"Oh, you definitely did. If he cheated on you once, he'll cheat again." I stood and grabbed my jacket. "I'm on my way."

"You don't have to. I'll be okay. I just thought you should know, that's all. The plan was to call you and tell you he's a bastard, but I guess it all becomes a little too real when you have to say it. I didn't intend to cry on you. I don't want to ruin your Christmas."

I grimaced. Harvey Walker had already done that, so what did one more drama matter. "You're not. I'll be there in an hour. Put the kettle on." At least at my mum's there would be a kettle. That was already an improvement on sitting here and staring at the wall. I grabbed the same bag I'd taken to Xander's and let myself out of the front door.

CHAPTER NINETEEN

Xander

It had taken less than five seconds after the door had closed in Ferris's wake to realize I didn't have his number. We'd never swapped numbers. Why would we? We'd been living in the same house. There'd been no need to call one another. So how the hell was I supposed to call him? Had he said it knowing it wasn't possible? Was it just a throwaway comment meant to disguise the fact he was done with me?

The thought had panic filling my insides as I made my slow way down the stairs, Ferris predictably nowhere to be seen by the time I eventually reached the bottom and wrenched the door open. Fuck! Now, what was I supposed to do? My first instinct was to go after him, but with me still on crutches and melting snow on the ground, it wasn't a good idea. Not to mention the fact that I had zero chance of catching him if he didn't want to be caught.

"Xander? Where are you?"

And then there was Harvey. In my kitchen. I took in a deep lungful of cold air before letting it out slowly. One thing at a time. I needed to deal with Harvey first, and then I could worry about Ferris. Letting the door close, I headed for the kitchen, Harvey turning his head to smile as I came through the door. I'd always liked his smile, but in comparison to Ferris's, Harvey's smile suddenly seemed just as fake as his tan.

I stopped dead at the sight of a reindeer antler poking out of a rubbish bag. Harvey had gathered up every single one, discarding them without even a moment's consideration of asking me first. Fury rose in me like lava in a volcano. Fury that I should have unleashed the moment I saw him. Life would have been far simpler if I'd simply shut the door in his face, or just not bothered answering it in the first place. Or… instead of being a spineless coward and trying to avoid confrontation, I could have introduced Ferris as my lover. Ferris would still be here, and I wouldn't be fighting a simmering rage that threatened to explode in a very unpleasant way if I didn't keep a lid on it.

I glared at Harvey. "Leave my stuff alone!" Ripping the bag open, I took all the reindeer out again and lined them up on the table. Over the last few days, Ferris had named them all, making the names increasingly more outlandish just to amuse me.

Harvey looked genuinely surprised. "You want them?"

"Of course, I want them. Why else do you think they're in my house?"

He shrugged, grimacing as he took a sip of his coffee. "We need to get some soya milk. You know what my stomach's like when I drink cow's milk. Can you go to the shop when you get a minute?" His gaze traveled slowly over me, pausing on my crutches. "Oh, I guess I should probably go."

"You think?" I didn't even attempt to hide my sarcasm. I'd spent two years in an on again off again relationship with Harvey Walker, and it was like someone had finally ripped my rose-tinted glasses off. He had good points. He could be extremely generous and attentive when he wanted to be, but he had far more bad points, like the fact he thought it was okay to not contact me for weeks and then just turn up on my doorstep acting like nothing was wrong.

I took a deep breath. "I've called you numerous times over the last few weeks. Why didn't you bother to answer any of them?"

Harvey looked slightly taken aback. "I've been busy. You know what its like when I'm working."

"Too busy to pick up the phone and return one of my calls, or to send a quick text asking how I was?"

His brow creased. "I'm sure I did."

"You didn't. Also…" I was warming up now. "You couldn't have left Switzerland any faster after my accident if the police had been after you. You were there one minute and gone the next with barely a word of farewell."

"I…" There was finally a trace of guilt on his handsome features. "I don't deal well with, you know"—he waved a hand down the length of my body—"illness and such like."

"And you think I do?"

Harvey shrugged.

I was suddenly done with the whole conversation. Hell, not just the conversation, the whole thing. Our relationship was more dead than the proverbial dormouse. I just needed him to understand that. "Anyway, when you left the way you did, and then didn't contact me, I made the assumption that 99.9 percent of the population would also have made, that we were over. And… over the last few weeks of zero communication I've realized that I'm okay with that. Really okay with it. We were on borrowed time anyway."

"Xander?"

I recognized the cajoling tone, knowing exactly where he was going with this, mainly because we'd been down the same road before. So many times that it probably needed resurfacing. Harvey thought he could wheedle his way back into my good books, that I'd agree to give things another go. I couldn't blame him, not when it had always worked for him before.

"We're over, Harvey." The words tasted so good in my mouth. "You can't stay here. You can't spend Christmas with me. I'm sorry you flew all the way to London, but well, you should have picked up the phone. It's a case of too little, too late, I'm afraid."

There was a moment of stunned silence where Harvey didn't seem to know what to do with my little speech, but it didn't last long, Harvey's eyes narrowing and his chin lifting. "I get it. This is about you and the nurse, isn't it?" He gestured at the line of reindeer, giving the closest one a little prod. I'd never wished for a reindeer to come alive and be capable of biting before, but I wished for it now. "I knew all this tat wasn't your style. I was beginning to worry you'd suffered brain damage from the fall. I guess the nurse has been fulfilling your every need. I wondered why he didn't seem very pleased to see me. I thought you'd just been badmouthing me."

"Yeah, me and... Ferris." I could hardly deny it, not when it was true. I wasn't going to let him get away with a dig like that without retaliating, though. "And what about you? How many men have kept your bed warm over the last few weeks, Harvey? I'm guessing at least a few." He didn't need to answer, the smile playing on his lips was answer enough. God, Mia had been so right about him. He'd always played around on me. I just hadn't wanted to see it. "Yeah, I thought so."

He placed his mug of half-drunk coffee on the table. "I guess I'll go and stay at a hotel then."

"I think that would be a good idea."

I didn't follow as he left the kitchen, staying where I was and listening to the telltale rustle of him putting his coat on. Then there was the squeak of suitcase wheels, followed by the front door opening and closing. And then silence. So much silence. Even when Ferris and I had been in different rooms, I'd usually been able to hear him moving around or humming a Christmas song.

I went into the living room first, the giraffe from the nativity scene seeming to have a distinctly accusatory look in his eye. Luke, Leia, and Han didn't seem very happy with the situation either. From there, I went to the spare room, standing in the doorway and scanning the room in case Ferris had left anything behind. If he'd left something, he might come back for it. But there was nothing. He'd even made the bed. Actually, he probably hadn't, had he? He'd been sleeping in my bed ever since the night we'd gone on a date. Our one and only date. And now, I didn't know whether there'd be any more, the thought triggering a dull ache in my chest.

Leaving the spare room, I went back to the kitchen where I'd left my phone and typed out a quick message.

Xander: *Miles, do you have Ferris's number?*

I stared at Harvey's half-drunk cup of coffee while I waited for the reply. There was a fly in it. Had that been there when he'd been drinking it? I hoped so. In fact, I hoped there'd been two and the other was currently trying to crawl its way back up his esophagus.

Miles: *Nope.*

I swore under my breath. I'd hoped it would be simple. I'd get Ferris's number from Miles. I'd call him, beg for his forgiveness and get him back where he should be—at my side, both annoying me and making me smile, usually at the same time.

Xander: *You met him. How can you not have his number?*

Miles: *Phil organized a meeting place for us. Anyway, why would you need his number? He's staying with you. Try talking to him. I find that works.*

Xander: *I don't suppose you'd agree NOT to ask questions? Can you get his number from Phil?*

Miles: *Nope. If you want me to go to the trouble of hassling people over Christmas for a number, there's no way I'm not going to be asking questions.*

I'd already known it was unlikely. Miles wasn't exactly known for keeping his nose out of my business. It was his job as my older brother and he tended to take it seriously.

Xander: *We had a thing. Harvey turned up. Ferris left. Yes, I am on my own. No, I don't need you to come back.*

A few minutes ticked by before I got a response from Miles.

Miles: *I see. I can't get a flight anyway. I just checked. I'm messaging Phil now.*

Another pause.

Miles: *He doesn't have it. Apparently, Ferris changed his number in the last couple of weeks. Phil's only got the old one. And he doesn't have his new address either. Sorry.*

I let my head *thunk* on the kitchen table, the impact sending Harvey's coffee, fly and all, splashing across it. *Fuck! Fuck! Fuck!* Now, what was I supposed to do? I watched as the fly, sensing freedom, slowly crawled away.

Miles: *Xander, you okay?*

Was I? I was a huge idiot, that was for sure. Every decision I'd made that day had been the wrong one. I shouldn't have opened the door. I shouldn't have introduced Ferris as just a nurse, and I shouldn't have let him walk away.

Xander: *Yeah, I'm fine. I'll find some other way of sorting it out.*

Miles: *Well, take care and I'll see you in a few days.*

I rang Mia. She answered on the third ring. "Hi, sweetheart."

I didn't bother wasting time on pleasantries. "Can you talk? I fucked up." I relayed the whole story to her, Mia listening quietly apart from interjecting with the odd question when she needed something clarifying. Silence met my retelling of events. "Say something."

"You're an idiot, Xander Cole."

I groaned. "I know that. I need to know how to fix things."

She let out a sigh. "So let me get this straight. You managed to start a torrid affair with someone without getting so much as a number or an address from them?"

"He was here. He was living in my house. I didn't need to."

"But he told you to call him when he left?"

"Yes!" I ran a hand through my hair. "But I don't know if he meant it or not."

"Hmm… How was he when he left? Was he angry?"

I thought about it. "Not really. He was more… resigned. Like he'd been waiting for something like this to happen."

"Okay." Mia made a clicking sound. She often did that when she was thinking. "One person can't be that difficult to track down. Let's think about what you know about him. You know he's a nurse. Where does he work?"

I closed my eyes in the hope it would help me to think. "I can't remember. He did mention the name of a hospital, but I can't remember which one. And even if I could, I can't remember whether it was the one he used to work at, or the one he's meant to be starting at."

"Jesus, Xander, what do you do when he's talking, just stare into his eyes and contemplate how handsome he is and all the things you want to do to him?"

Pretty much! I wasn't going to admit that to her, though. "I listen to him."

"Not very well apparently."

"In my defense, that conversation was post-orgasm. We'd just—"

"Stop. I don't need to know, thank you very much."

I clicked my fingers. "Dorothy."

"Xander, I don't think now is the time to start extolling the virtues of *The Wizard of Oz*. I know you love the film and you're a big fan of the flying monkeys, but they're not going to help you track down Ferris."

"No! Dorothy was an ex-patient of Ferris's. We went round for tea. I think I can remember roughly where she lived. I'd definitely recognize the house if I saw it again. She'd be able to tell me the name of the hospital where he used to work. And the ward as well. Someone there's got to have his contact details. He said he was still going to a party with his old work colleagues, so he's still in touch with them." *The party!* All the synapses in my brain fired at the same time. "*And...* I know where Ferris is going to be on New Year's Eve. He's going to be at a party at the Walrus Bar."

"Yeah?" I could hear the smile in Mia's voice. "Then I guess you have a plan of action, after all. I hope you get your man, Xan. I really do."

So did I. At least I felt more positive than I had before I'd called her. It was just unfortunate that New Year's Eve was such a long way away. But if I could track down Dorothy before that, I wouldn't have to worry about it.

CHAPTER TWENTY

Ferris

December 28ᵗʰ

Christmas had gone about as well as you could expect when two people were both miserable and trying to make the best of it. In other words, not that well at all, my mum and I both taking it in turns to slip into a pit of depression that the other person would have to drag them out of. Barry had turned up twice, once on Christmas Day, and then again the previous day. He'd bellowed words of remorse through the letterbox of the door that my mum had refused to open, begging for forgiveness for what he'd called "a stupid error of judgment."

At least he'd tried, which was more than Xander had done. He hadn't called. He hadn't messaged. I'd heard absolutely nothing from him. And it hurt. A lot. I'd wanted something, even if it was just a half-hearted apology for the way things had ended between us.

My mum took the seat across from me at the kitchen table, pushing a plate of carrot cake and a fork in my direction. I took both. Xander would have liked the cake. I cursed myself. I had to stop doing that. It was like everything I saw, I now looked at through a lens of what Xander would have had to say about it. If I heard a Christmas song, it was about how much he would have hated it. Whether he would have ranked it above or below "Do they know it's Christmas," which he'd described as "unnecessarily confusing, given the number of different singers and the fact there were two different versions of it." If I ate anything, would Xander have liked it? If I watched anything on TV, had Xander ever watched the program? I was obsessed.

I lifted a piece of carrot cake to my mouth and chewed. I couldn't really taste it, but at least it gave me something to do. Deep down, I knew the truth. I wasn't obsessed. I was in love. Although, maybe they were the same thing. I'd not only mixed business and pleasure, but I'd done the stupidest thing I could and I'd fallen for him.

And what did I have to show for it? Nothing but memories and regrets about what could have been, numerous what ifs floating through my head at regular intervals. What if Harvey hadn't turned up when he had? What if I hadn't left and I'd stood my ground? What if I'd told Harvey that I'd been sleeping with Xander? Actually, there were quite a few things I regretted not having said to Harvey Walker. I'd like to have told him he didn't deserve to be with Xander after dumping him in Switzerland for work. What kind of man chose taking photos over his boyfriend? And if that question had made him struggle for adjectives to describe himself, I'd have been happy to provide a few, starting with selfish and uncaring and probably rounding them off with twat for good measure.

But... none of that had happened. So it was pointless to dwell on it. I'd made my decision and there was no turning back time and getting to do things differently. Life didn't work like that.

"Aren't you going to open it?"

"Huh?" I lifted my head to find my mum staring at the wrapped box I had next to me on the table. I'd been running my fingers over the brightly colored ribbons without conscious thought. "No... it's not for me." At her raised eyebrow, I elaborated. "It was for Xander. We'd agreed not to buy each other presents, but I saw this and I couldn't resist. It would have made him laugh."

"What is it?"

"It's a..." I let the colored ribbons trail through my fingers one more time. "It's a grumpy bear Christmas ornament. The bear's wearing a sling."

Lines appeared on my mum's forehead. "Why is that funny?"

"Because its basically him. He would have got it."

She nodded. "You could still give it to him."

I shook my head. "He was supposed to call. I left the ball in his court. Besides, it's just a stupid ornament."

My mum tucked a piece of hair behind her ear. "You could go round there. Even if you don't want to give him the present, you could say you just wanted to check how he is. That's a perfectly valid excuse. He was your patient, after all."

I thought about it. I imagined just casually turning up there. Xander opening the door to me would be like coming full circle. And then I imagined Harvey appearing in the background. He'd probably be in a towel and would have a serious case of bedhead because the two of them had barely gotten out of bed over Christmas. Thinking about the two of them together made me want to vomit. It was bad enough imagining it. I didn't need to see it. I shook my head. "No. He's got my number if he wants to talk to me."

My mum sighed and I went back to picking at my carrot cake. Miles would be back from Spain by now. I wondered what he'd made of finding me gone and Harvey there instead. I guessed I'd never know.

A commotion broke out in the backyard, my mum and I both rising from our chairs. It didn't take a genius to work out what had caused it. Barry was apparently more persistent than I'd given him credit for. But then, I'd heard he'd been sleeping in his car, so whether it was my mum he was unwilling to give up, or the roof over his head was very much up for debate.

He'd made it to the back door by the time we reached the kitchen window. We both watched as he lifted his fists to hammer on it. My mum let out a long sigh. "He's going to upset the neighbors."

"Let him. Maybe they'll call the police if we're lucky. At least then we'll get a rest from him."

"Laura, I know you're in there. Open up. I just want to talk."

The shout was so loud that I jumped. Barry must have had his face pressed right up against the door. I shook my head. "Don't open it. You don't have to."

My mum looked at the door and then at me, and then back to the door, clearly conflicted. "I should at least talk to him. He deserves to have his say."

"He doesn't deserve any such thing."

"He's not going to stop until I do."

"He's—"

But I was too late, my mum already flicking the lock back and pulling the door open. I shrank back, figuring it was better for everyone concerned if Barry didn't know I was there. Hopefully, she wouldn't go as far as to invite him in.

"Barry."

"Laura."

And then they were both silent. I guess at this rate I didn't have anything to worry about in terms of a big emotional reunion. Another minute ticked slowly by before Barry finally seemed to remember his purpose in being there. "I messed up. I know I did." I nodded profusely along with him. "But... we had a really good thing going." I shook my head just as emphatically as I'd nodded. My mum stayed silent. She wasn't buying this crap, was she? "I made *one* mistake. And I know it was a big one, and it shouldn't have happened, but I can promise you that it won't happen again. Just give me another chance, that's all I ask. And I'll make it up to you. I am *so* sorry that it happened, but I've learnt my lesson. I've realized how important you are to me, and how stupid I was to ever put that at risk."

I waited for my mum to tell him where he could stick his apologies, but all that came out of her mouth was, "I wish I could believe you."

Crap! I could see the reunion on the horizon. Even if it wasn't today, it would be somewhere down the line—a few days or a few weeks from now. Was this what it had been like for Xander? His good intentions and supposed ambivalence toward Harvey crumbling away at a few well-chosen words. I might not have done enough to save him, but I wasn't about to make the same mistake twice.

I stepped forward, Barry's eyes widening as I appeared at my mum's back. "Ferris, I didn't know you were here. Do you think you could give us a bit of space so we can talk in private? Your mum and I have got a lot to discuss."

I let out a snort. "That's about as likely as me growing wings and flying down the street." I crossed my arms over my chest. "I knew you'd cheat eventually, but I figured it would be with a guy, not with another woman."

My mum's brow furrowed. "What are you talking about?"

I kept my gaze fixed on Barry. "Do you want to tell her, or shall I?"

Barry laughed, but it wasn't that convincing. "Tell her what?"

My mum turned to me, her frown growing more pronounced. "Yes Ferris, tell me what?"

"Barry"—I pointed at him for maximum effect—"has something of a roving eye. Always has done. And many is the time that it's roved in my direction when you've been looking the other way."

My mum looked even more confused. "I don't understand what you're saying."

Barry made a sound of disdain. "He's making stuff up."

That comment had my blood boiling. Or maybe it was all the pent-up frustration from what had happened with Xander. Whatever it was, I let rip. "Oh really. So you didn't keep constantly undressing me with your eyes? You didn't make little comments and sexual innuendoes every time Mum left the room? That was in my head, was it? What was it you said the last time, when I was contemplating staying here? Oh, that was it, you offered to keep my bed warm for me." I let my gaze trail slowly down his body, not bothering to hide my blatant disgust for him. "As if."

Barry laughed, but it lacked conviction. "It's not—"

My mum didn't let him finish. "I think you should go. I've obviously been blind to a lot of things that have been going on right under my nose."

"Laura, I…"

She closed the door in his face and I had to suppress the desire to cheer. "You're doing the right thing. I know it hurts at the moment, but in the long-term it will be far better."

She turned slowly to face me. "He was coming on to you?"

I couldn't hold back my wince. "Yeah."

"For how long?"

I shrugged. "A while." It sounded better than saying from the first time I'd met him. Actually, it was probably the third or fourth time. I seemed to remember him being on his best behavior for the first few occasions.

"And you didn't tell me?"

The accusation in my mum's voice was clear. As was the hurt written all over her face. "I just…" It was the same conversation I'd had with Xander. "You were happy. Who was I to take that away from you?"

"So… you let me look like an idiot instead, shacked up with a man who apparently wanted to sleep with the barmaid down the road *and* my own son."

There was no defense I could give. She turned away. "Mum, I…"

She shook her head. "I could do with some time on my own. It's been lovely to have you here over Christmas, but I know you need to sort your new flat out."

"I can stay longer."

"You don't need to." She managed a smile, but it only lasted a couple of seconds. Her dismissal didn't come as a surprise. I'd always known that by not telling her, I was running the risk of her being more upset at a later date if the truth came out. But she'd needed to know. The least I could do though, was let her lick her wounds in private.

I was packing my bag when my phone rang. My heart leapt, the same way it had every other time since I'd left Xander's house. And just like every other time, it wasn't him and I found myself mumbling a "hello" to my old work colleague, Emma, instead.

She sounded far happier than I was. "Four days to party time!"

"What?"

She laughed. "New Year's Eve, dummy. The party."

I shifted my phone to the opposite ear. "Yeah, course."

"You are coming. You said you would."

I had, but that was before Xander, and before all the Barry drama. I felt like a wrung-out dishcloth. I was hardly going to be the life and soul of the party. "I don't know. I haven't unpacked yet, and I'm not really in the mood to celebrate."

"You have to come! Everyone will be so upset if you're not there. Tell me you'll be there."

I let out a breath. I tried to imagine myself at the New Year party. It would be all heaving bodies and drunken people. Drunken people who'd be intent on finding someone to kiss at midnight. I couldn't imagine wanting to kiss anyone but

Xander. But he'd be at home kissing Harvey. A party sounded like absolute hell on earth. "I'll see. I'm not promising anything."

CHAPTER TWENTY-ONE

Xander

New Year's Eve

The car seat squeaked as Miles turned to face me, his fingers tapping out a rhythm I didn't recognize on the steering wheel. "Are you sure you don't want me to come in with you?"

I shook my head. "I don't need my brother holding my hand."

He snorted. "I was thinking more along the lines of physical help rather than emotional help." He gestured at the cane propped up against the seat. "Especially seeing as you were so insistent on using that instead of the crutches. Given that its snowed again, I think the crutches would have been safer."

"I'll be fine." I wasn't fine. I was a nervous wreck. My plan to get Ferris's location from Dorothy had started well. The cab driver had been surprisingly patient as I'd gotten him to drive round and round the streets until I'd finally recognized Dorothy's house from the flowered curtains hung at the window. Unfortunately, my luck had ended at that point. I'd knocked for at least ten minutes, the cab driver happy to sit and watch the meter run, but nobody had come to the door. In the end, there'd been no other option but to admit defeat and return home, no closer to finding Ferris than I'd been when I'd set out.

This was the only lead I had left, given Ferris had invited me to the party before everything had blown up in my face courtesy of Harvey. Actually, I couldn't really blame Harvey, could I? All it would have taken was one text to end things properly. I should have done that the moment I'd started sleeping with Ferris.

I stared out of the window at The Walrus Bar. It was lucky the place had such a distinctive name. Anything more generic and I doubted I would have remembered it. Even from the road, I could tell there was definitely a party going on inside. One that included a fair few people by the looks of it.

There were numerous things that could go wrong with my plan. Everything hinged on Ferris actually attending the party, but he could have changed his mind or gotten a better offer. And even if he was here, I might not be able to find him. Or I might find him and he wouldn't want to speak to me.

It might only have been just over a week since I'd last seen him but a lot could happen in that time. And those days had felt like a month to me, Miles returning from Spain to find me moping around the house. I missed Ferris. I missed having breakfast with him in the morning. I missed him winding me up. I missed everything about him. I even missed having him there when I did my damn exercises. The same damn exercises that I'd kept up religiously, imagining Ferris's voice in my head if I so much as missed a day.

Miles coughed, and I turned to stare at him. "What?"

He raised his eyebrows. "You do realize that in order to go inside, you have to actually leave the car."

I sighed. "Yes, I do realize that. Sorry, I didn't know you had a hot date. I thought you were just dropping me off and then going back to mine to drink hot chocolate and watch shit TV."

He clasped a hand to his chest. "Ouch! That's mean. And I'll have you know that it's very expensive hot chocolate and if I'm really pushing the boat out, I might put some Kahlua in it."

"Wow! Don't get too wild and crazy."

"I'll try not to." He tapped out another rhythm on the steering wheel, this one more rapid. "Are you sure you don't want me to wait? I don't mind."

I shook my head. Getting Miles to wait was tantamount to admitting the night might have a conclusion that wasn't in my favor. "If it all goes tits up, I'll call a cab." I checked my watch. It was already after nine—traffic, weather, and Miles's dithering all playing a part in a later arrival than I'd been hoping for. What if Ferris had been here, but had already gone home. But then who went to a New Year's Eve party and left before midnight?

"We can track him down some other way, you know. I'm sure Phil can get hold of his new number. You just need to wait. That might be better than seeking him out at a party. It's a bit"—Miles threw his hands up in the air—"you know, a bit dramatic if you ask me."

I smiled. "It's Ferris. He likes drama." I grabbed the cane, reaching for the door handle. "Right! Wish me luck."

"Good luck. If you do need me to pick you up, then…"

The last part of my brother's speech was lost as I slammed the door shut, but I got the gist. I made my slow and careful way over to the door of the bar, avoiding as many patches of snow as I could. A couple standing outside smoking cast curious glances in my direction. I guessed they weren't used to seeing someone come out partying with a cane. I'd changed my mind at least three or four times about whether to get dressed up or not, but in the end, I'd decided that as well as blending in better it was in my best interests to look my best. Luckily, there was no one standing guard at the door to stop uninvited guests from sneaking in.

A blare of a car horn came from behind me, Miles lifting his hand in a wave before driving off. I waved back, waiting until the car was out of sight before stepping through the door. It was dark inside and crammed with people, my heart skipping a beat at the thought of trying to find Ferris in the crowd. It was also very loud, Lady Gaga and Ariana Grande singing about "teardrops on their face" before the dance beat kicked in. I scanned the crowd, hoping to catch sight of a familiar dark head, but of course it was never going to be that easy.

For the next forty-five minutes, I said more "Excuse me's" and "Sorry's" than I'd ever said before in my life. Walking with a cane was difficult. Navigating crowds with it was nigh on impossible. I'd stopped a few people, concentrating on those that didn't look like they were already three sheets to the wind, asking if they knew Ferris. They all knew who he was, but none of them seemed to recall whether they'd seen him tonight.

My hip throbbing, I made a detour to the bar and leaned against it, considering whether the desire for painkillers when I got home outweighed the urge to have a beer. In the end, I went for water. If I did manage to track Ferris down, I wanted a relatively clear head. I was already after a second chance. I didn't want to find myself in the position of angling for a third. I continually scanned the mass of heaving bodies, but it was too dark and too crowded to be able to make out much. It was like looking for the proverbial needle in a haystack. I wasn't going to give up, though. Not until the bar was about to close and I was the last person left.

Someone slid in next to me and I automatically turned my head their way. The blond-haired man offered me a wink. "Hey." He pointed at my glass. "Please tell me that's neat vodka and not water."

"It's water." I had to shout to be heard over the music.

He pulled a face. "Want me to buy you something more interesting?"

I shook my head.

"What's your name?"

"Xander."

"Xander!" He said it like I'd said something impressive. "Unusual name."

I shrugged.

"My name's Dr. Murphy, but you can call me Chris."

Was I meant to be impressed? I bit my tongue against the urge to tell him I didn't intend to call him anything.

He studied my face. "Where do you work in the hospital? I've never seen you. I would definitely have remembered you."

I ignored the question as I drained the last of my water. "Do you know Ferris? Ferris Night?"

His nose wrinkled. "The annoying nurse?"

I laughed. "Yeah, the annoying nurse. Have you seen him tonight?"

He tipped his head to one side, considering me for far longer than the question required. "Yeah, I saw him earlier. He was surrounded by his usual bunch of sycophants."

Ferris was here. A mixture of relief and anticipation had my heart hammering against my ribs. "Where was he?"

Chris let out a sigh, finally seeming to get the message that I wasn't remotely interested in him. He was good-looking, but he wasn't Ferris. He lifted a finger to point up. "Second floor."

There was another floor. Jesus! No wonder I hadn't had any luck finding him. "Thanks." I pushed myself away from the bar before pausing. "Where are the stairs?"

He gestured toward the back of the room. "Behind the Christmas tree."

Of course it was—the obstructive bastard. It just went to prove my point that they had a lot to answer for. I made my way over there, the majority of the people in the crowd oblivious to my efforts to navigate my way through them. When I eventually reached the stairs, I needed to stop for a breather before I tackled them.

At the top, was an almost identical room to the one below: bar, dancefloor, throng of people—no sign of Ferris. It was difficult to know where to start as I scanned the room. I couldn't see him by the bar. There were a few tables with people seated, but I couldn't see him there either. Would he be dancing? It seemed as good a place as any to start. I could do a circuit and see if I could spot him.

I turned too fast, my cane slipping on a patch of damp where someone had presumably spilled their drink. The world slowed, the imminent likelihood of ending up in a heap on the floor sending a surge of adrenaline through my body. But then arms wrapped around me from behind, steadying me and averting disaster while I regained my balance. I took a deep breath to calm my racing heart. "Thank you."

Once I was sure I could remain upright, I turned to thank my savior properly, only to find myself staring into a very familiar face indeed. A million emotions all started competing with each other, the rush of intensity leaving me incapable of speech.

Ferris's brow furrowed as he stared at me as if I was some sort of apparition. "Xander! What the hell are you doing here? As far as I'm aware you've never worked for St Thomas's. Got some sort of deep, dark secret you want to share? Do you moonlight as a hospital porter on the weekends?"

I shook my head, swallowing in an attempt to find my voice. "I was looking for you. You told me you'd be here. You invited me, remember."

Ferris didn't say anything, his face giving absolutely nothing away. Was he pleased to see me? Was he angry that I was here? I needed to say something that mattered, something that would fix this chasm between us. The obvious words came bursting out of me like water from a geyser. "I love you." There, I'd said it. It felt good to put the words out there. This was where Ferris would sweep me into his arms and everything would be okay.

Ferris leaned forward. "What? I can't hear you over the music."

Unfortunately, my declaration had coincided with the chorus kicking in. I said it again, this time louder. Ferris shook his head, putting his hand behind his ear in the universal sign for "I can't hear you."

"I said, I LOVE YOU!" My third declaration coincided with the end of the song, the last strains dying away just as I screamed the words. Everyone in a five-mile radius turned to look at me. At least that was what it felt like. I'd never really understood the saying about someone wanting the floor to open up and swallow them before, but now, with my cheeks the appropriate heat of the center of the Earth, I understood it only too well.

And Ferris. Well, Ferris was no help at all. He was just staring at me with his mouth hanging open. The expression on his face wouldn't have been out of place if I'd just announced that I was a serial killer and I'd decided to make him my next victim.

I shouldn't have come here. I should have taken a vow of abstinence and joined a monastery instead. Did people still do that? I'd have to look into it. One of the photographers—not Harvey—had once said I could make any clothes look good. I doubted he'd been thinking about a cassock at the time, but I'd do my best to make it work. Were monks allowed to accessorize? Sometimes a belt could make the world of difference. Yeah, I'd be the monk with the snazzy belts.

Ferris finally seemed to snap out of it. He grabbed my arm and led me... Actually, I didn't know where he was leading me, but I didn't particularly care, as long as it was away from the crowd of people who were still staring like they had absolutely nothing better to do with their lives than gawp at some idiot who'd just declared his feelings in the most obnoxious way possible.

And then we were stepping into a lounge, with sofas and soft chairs, the music dulling to nothing more than a dull thud as the door swung shut behind us. I collapsed into the nearest chair, closed my eyes and let out a breath. Except… what was that noise? Was Ferris laughing? I opened my eyes to find him almost doubled over, looking like he could hardly breathe. "What's so funny?"

It took him a good minute to get himself back under control. "You've got to admit that was hilarious."

I narrowed my eyes at him. "Do I look like I'm laughing?"

Ferris grabbed a chair and pulled it diagonal to mine, our knees almost touching. At least he'd stopped laughing. "You're walking better."

"I was. I think I've overdone it, though. I'm probably going to pay for it tomorrow. I'll need a nurse." Jesus! That was cheesy. And completely unnecessary given that I'd already told him I loved him. I'd said I loved him and he'd said… nothing. Didn't a confession like that deserve at least some sort of response? "I meant it, you know."

"Meant what?"

"What I said out there… three times."

Ferris rubbed a hand over his face. "So why didn't you call? I've been waiting for you to call. It's been eight days, Xander. I know it has because I counted them. Eight *long* days."

I stared at him. Was he serious? "How was I suppose to call when I didn't have your number?"

"I left it for you."

"Where?"

"In the spare room. I wouldn't just walk out without leaving you a way of contacting me."

I struggled to wrap my head around what he'd just said. Was that possible? I'd gone in there hoping he'd left something behind? Except, I'd only stood in the doorway, hadn't I? I could have missed it. Besides, what reason did Ferris have to lie. Had we really spent eight days apart when we hadn't needed to? "Christ! I've been trying to track you down. I've had Miles harassing Phil for your number, only to find out that you apparently changed it, and I even tried to go and see Dorothy, figuring she could at least tell me what hospital you used to work at and I could take it from there. Only she didn't answer the door."

"She's back in hospital."

"Oh!"

Ferris let out a sigh. "When you didn't call, I assumed you and Harvey had patched things up."

I pulled a face. "Hardly. I kicked his ass out about five minutes after you left."

He raised an eyebrow. "That soon! What did he do to deserve that?"

"Apart from be himself… he put Princess Bebopalula and the rest of the reindeer in a rubbish bag."

"Bastard! What did she ever do to him?"

"Exactly."

Ferris moved his chair closer until our knees pressed together, the simple touch sending an electric thrill through me. "I should have stayed."

I shook my head. "I don't blame you for having doubts, and for feeling like you had to leave. I've got to take some responsibility. If I'd sent one simple text message to Harvey stating it was over, he wouldn't have jumped on a plane and shown up at my door. And I should have introduced you as my…"

"Boyfriend?"

"Are you? I mean, were you? It wasn't just that I was avoiding confrontation. We hadn't put a label on our relationship, so I didn't want to be presumptuous."

Ferris smiled, the familiar sight doing strange things to my insides after not having seen it for so long. "I thought that's where we were heading. I wouldn't have slept with you, if not."

"Good to know." I reached out and took his hand, pulling it onto my lap, our gazes locked together. "I've told you how I feel. What about you?"

The seconds that ticked by might as well have been years. "Can you say it again?"

I laughed. "Shouting it in front of hundreds of people wasn't enough for you? How many people are here anyway? I thought this was a work thing."

Ferris stroked his thumb over my knuckle. "It's a big hospital."

I nodded as I leaned forward. "I know we've only known each other a few weeks, but… I do, I love you."

Ferris's answering smile was bright enough to light up the entire room. "I love you too."

My chest was so full of emotion I could barely breathe. "You do. Seriously? You're not just saying that."

Ferris shook his head. "I'm not just saying that."

I stared at our clasped hands, sudden doubts forcing their way into my brain. "I travel a lot. Work can take me out of the country frequently. I won't always be around." I lifted my head and risked a glance at him.

He looked amused as he cocked his head to one side. "So… you tell me you love me, and now you're telling me all the reasons we shouldn't be together. I'm getting some majorly mixed signals here, Xander."

"I'm not trying to put you off. I just want to be realistic and point out that I'm hardly the perfect catch."

Ferris snorted. "Oh, I already know that."

I reared back. "Hey! What's wrong with me?"

"Where do I start?" Ferris held up his hand as if he was about to start ticking things off. "Grumpy in the morning. Actually, strike that, it can be any time of day. Anti-Christmas. No appreciation of snow. Too good a metabolism, which makes me jealous. Completely oblivious to someone cheating at cards, unless it's made really obvious. Absolutely—"

I shut him up the best way I knew how, by kissing him. It had been way too long since I'd felt his lips on mine. He tasted of vodka and Ferris, and it was like falling back into the best habit imaginable. When we finally came up for air, we were both smiling. I stood, using the side of the chair for balance. "Dance with me."

Ferris stared at me like I'd grown an extra head. "You don't dance. You told me that."

I tugged him to his feet. "I also told you that I wasn't coming to this party."

His laugh was a low chuckle in his throat. "That's true."

He pulled me in close, and I let go of the cane to wind my arms around his neck. "If you let me go, I'll probably fall on the floor."

"Don't tempt me."

It felt good to have Ferris in my arms again as we swayed together. Really good.

His lips ghosted over my neck, coming to rest against my ear. "What are we dancing to?"

It was a good point. We could hear the thump of the music, but it wasn't clear enough to make head nor tail of what it was. "I don't know."

Ferris turned his head to brush a kiss over my jaw. "Not a problem. I can provide the music. He made a show out of clearing his throat before launching into Mariah Carey. "I don't want a lot for Christmas. There is just one thing I need. I don't care about the presents underneath the Christmas tree."

I rolled my eyes. "It had to be that, didn't it? You do know that Christmas is over."

Ferris pulled back to give me a mock glare. "Sshh. I'm just getting to the good bit." He held my gaze as he carried on singing. "I just want you for my own. More than you could ever know. Make my wish come true." He gave a dramatic pause before continuing. "All I want for Christmas is you-ooh."

I couldn't help but smile. I might not like the song, but I was definitely on board with the sentiment. "You got me. Going to come home with me?" I came back to Earth with a sudden bump. "Oh, wait. You're here with friends. You can't just run out on them."

Ferris arched an eyebrow. "Can't I? You just watch me. I think they'll understand, given that they all witnessed you shouting in my face that you love me."

"Oh God!" I hid my burning cheek in his shoulder.

Ferris chuckled. "I've got to tell you, Xander, that if we're in this for the long run, you've got to work on your romance. You know, soft words and candlelight are more traditional. What you did was more the heavy metal version."

"I'm not gonna say it again."

Ferris squeezed me tighter. "Yeah, you will."

He was right as usual. I would.

CHAPTER TWENTY-TWO

Ferris

I checked my watch as the cab drew to a halt outside Xander's oh so familiar house. It seemed strange to see it again, but then it had been a strange night. I might have bowed to pressure to attend the New Year's Eve party, but it had been like slipping on a mask with a permanent smile etched on it, when all I'd really wanted to do was stay home, eat ice-cream and wallow amongst all the boxes that I still hadn't unpacked.

My friends hadn't seemed to notice that my happiness was all a front, which meant I was either a better actor than I thought I was, or I needed new friends. I'd been in the process of pondering how to slip away without anyone noticing when

someone had literally fallen into my arms. Despite knowing that the accident was likely to be the result of too much alcohol imbibed in a short time, years of instinct honed on the wards had had me swooping to the rescue.

And who had I rescued? Well, that had been the kicker. None other than Xander Cole. Right there in front of me. Dressed up. Minus the crutches, and looking good enough to eat. And shouting declarations of love in my face to boot. I had to admit to giving serious thought to the possibility of someone having slipped something in my drink.

Xander paid the fare and then got out of the car, leaning on his cane with one hand while he held the other out to me. I took it gladly. The world suddenly seemed full of possibilities, when only a few hours ago it had seemed drained of any color. He kept hold of my hand as we made our way up the path toward the door. We paused for a moment by the inflatable snowman, its massive body bobbing slightly in the breeze. "Still here, then."

Xander aimed a look my way. "*You're* getting rid of the Christmas decorations."

I smirked. "Oh, so that's why you came to look for me, is it?"

Xander laughed as he slid his key in the lock. "Too right, it is. The fact I can't get you out of my head was just secondary. By the way, Miles took one look at the Christmas decorations when he got back and thought I'd gone insane."

"Did he?" I wasn't really thinking about Miles. I was still focusing on the part where Xander had said he couldn't get me out of his head, a warm glow spreading through my chest. We'd been stupid. We'd spent the last week apart, both pining for each other, when we could have been together. There was definitely a lesson there about direct communication rather than leaving people notes and making assumptions about what was going on instead of finding out the truth. If I'd swallowed my pride and done what my mum had suggested and turned up at Xander's door, this could all have been sorted days ago.

I followed Xander into the house, our fingers still interlocked, neither of us seeming to want to let go. Apart from the reindeer that had taken up a security role by the bottom of the stairs, everything else was exactly the same.

Xander came to a stop by the open doorway of the living room, Miles lifting his head from the book he'd been reading. He smirked as his gaze dropped to our joined hands. "I guess you found him then, and you sorted things out." He turned to me with a twinkle in his eye. "Thank God for that. I couldn't take any more of Xander's long silences, or the way he just sat and stared into space for hours with a look of longing on his face."

Xander's fingers twitched in mine. "I wasn't that bad."

Miles snorted. "Course you weren't." He closed his book. "Is this where I need to make myself scarce so that you two can have an emotional reunion?"

Xander shook his head. "No, we're going upstairs."

I leaned my head against his shoulder. "Oh, are we? That's a bit presumptuous, isn't it? I'm not that easy, you know."

Xander raised an eyebrow. "Yeah, you are."

I thought about it before nodding. "Yeah, I am. For you, anyway."

Miles rolled his eyes and opened his book again, but he was smiling. "Told you, you'd be good for my brother."

I laughed. He had. "You didn't say he'd be just as good for me, though."

He aimed a wink in my direction. "I'm not the oracle. I can't know everything."

Xander tugged me away, and we made our way up the stairs. At the top, he veered off toward the spare room. I followed, reaching the door to find him standing in the middle of the room with a puzzled look on his face. "Where did you leave it?"

Ah, the note. I stepped inside. "Do you think I'm making it up?"

"No, I believe you, but it's going to annoy me if I can't solve the mystery of where it got to."

I went over to the chest of drawers, frowning as I ran my hand over its empty surface. "Here, but..." Had Harvey found it? It wasn't like he would have wanted Xander to have a way of communicating with me. I wouldn't have put it past the snakey bastard to have destroyed it. Except Xander had said he'd kicked Harvey out not long after I'd left so when would he have had the chance? I peered down the back of the drawers, the answer very quickly making itself known as I spotted the thinnest sliver of paper. I pulled it out with a flourish and held it out to Xander. "There."

He took it and read it, his gaze lifting to mine with an amused look in his eye. "Love Ferris? You said it first."

I snorted. "Bollocks, I did. What did you expect me to write, yours sincerely? Besides, I didn't shout it at a hundred decibels. Nothing is ever going to beat that." Xander folded the note neatly and put it in his pocket. I quirked an eyebrow at him. "You're keeping it?"

Xander lifted his head with a smile. "I still don't have your number."

I held out my hand. "Give me your phone."

Xander was surprisingly obedient in doing as I asked, unlocking it first before handing it over. I keyed my number into his phone and then pressed call, a rousing instrumental version of "Jingle Bells" erupting from my pocket. "There. Now, can we *please* go to your room."

Xander turned and made off down the hallway. I decided I could get used to this version of him as I followed. Although, I had no doubt he was only doing as he was told because he wanted the same thing I did.

The bedroom door closed behind us and we were suddenly in each other's arms, kissing as if our very lives depended on it. I tore at his clothes, needing bare skin against mine, Xander's hands doing the same. Things caught on elbows and knees, both of us working in tandem to free them. My phone slipped out of my pocket and fell to the floor, but I didn't care. All I cared about was hot skin and the slide of Xander's tongue against mine.

This wasn't like the other times we'd had sex. The key thing then, had always been being careful. It had been the gradual burn of teasing kindling to full heat. Whereas this was like an inferno raging out of control. If this was what eight days separation did to us, I was already fearful of the times Xander would have to travel for work.

Hands landed on my chest, the sudden jolt sending me tumbling backwards onto the bed. I sprawled there, staring up at the magnificent sight of a naked and very aroused Xander. A small chink of memory burrowed its way into my skull. Why hadn't we done it like this before? Oh, that's right—the small matter of Xander's pelvis. "Don't hurt yourself."

He raised an eyebrow. "Not intending to. I do have a nurse on standby, though."

"Is that right? That must be handy."

"Oh, it is."

He crawled up the length of my body, my thighs automatically parting to allow him to lie between them. "Are you going to fuck me?"

His tongue laved my left nipple, teasing it into a tight bud, the sensation making my cock throb. "I'm going to try?" Xander laughed, his breath ghosting across my chest. "Isn't that what every man dreams of hearing? That I'm going to *try* and fuck you? Welcome to my bed, Ferris, where dreams turn into nightmares."

Chuckling, I pulled him up for a kiss. "Never. I'm sure your attempt will be ten times better than anyone else can manage." I slid my hands down his back, filling my palms with the taut muscular globes of Xander's ass. "How's your pelvis?"

Xander ground himself against me, shifting slightly so that cock met cock in a slide that felt so damn good that it was all I could do not to growl. "Still there. Still attached. Still functional."

"Functional! You know all the sexy words to get me going in bed."

I swallowed Xander's laugh by recapturing his lips, the two of us quickly becoming reacquainted with each other's bodies—lips, tongues, and hands working together to drive us both crazy until we were both desperate to come. Not wanting Xander to strain himself, I got the condom. I rolled it on him too. Although, that last bit was more about speed than anything else.

It was hard to say who'd taken the lead after that, but when Xander went to move forward, I stopped him. The risk was too high of him damaging himself. I didn't need him to prove anything. Instead, I straddled him, throwing my head back as I sank down onto him, careful to keep most of my weight off him as I rode him.

He watched me, his eyes pools of green fire as I set a rhythm that worked for both of us, each time I took him inside me driving both of us closer to orgasm.

Neither of us were interested in making it last. We had the rest of our lives for that, the knowledge making the impending orgasm twice as sweet. Wrapping a hand around my cock, I stroked it in time with the undulation of my hips. Xander came first, his groan of completion and the spasms coursing through his body sending me hurtling to join him, pure pleasure replacing conscious thought.

It took a while to come down from the orgasm. Once I could move, I got rid of the condom before hurrying back to Xander and snuggling into his side, Xander lifting his arm to make it easier. I pulled him closer. "I saw fireworks. Well, I heard them. That's never happened before."

Xander laughed against my neck. "Much as I'd like to take the credit for that. I think you'll find it passed midnight and they were actual fireworks."

"Really?" I lifted my head so that I could see the clock on Xander's nightstand. "12:05. Huh, I guess you're right. And there was I thinking you had a magic cock." I turned my head to kiss Xander's forehead. "Happy New Year."

He rolled onto his side so that his head rested on my chest and I wrapped my arm around his waist. "Same to you."

I kissed the top of his head. It was hard to believe that after the misery of the last few days I was in bed with Xander Cole, but I was. And he was all mine. "I've got to tell you, that's the best orgasm I've had all year."

The only response I got was a snort.

I ran my fingers through his hair and he looked up, ensnaring me in that green gaze that I loved so much. "How was your Christmas?"

I sighed. "The shit hit the fan with Barry. He got caught cheating on my mum. Big surprise. We couldn't go a couple of days without him popping up and wangling for a reconciliation. My mum had gotten to the point where she'd started wavering, so…"

"You threw yourself under the bus and told her what a low-life he really was."

"Yeah."

Xander grimaced. "And how did she take it?"

"Well, she believed me. And it did the trick of not letting Mr. Slimy claw himself back into her good books. But she was understandably upset. She still is. She'll get over it. She just needs a bit of time."

Xander looked thoughtful. "You should distract her with something, like… I don't know, introducing her to your new boyfriend or something."

I smiled. "Would you be up for that, meeting my mum?"

"Of course. I want to meet everyone in your life."

My smile grew broader. "How about your Christmas?"

Xander's smile was sad. "Lonely and full of regret."

I lifted my head so I could see him properly. "Did you do your exercises?"

His mouth dropped open, and he dug his fingers into my ribs. "Seriously? I tell you how utterly miserable I've been, and that's what you want to know. I knew you were a slave driver, but I didn't realize quite how much of one you were. Yeah, I did my exercises through the tears. Happy now?"

I let my head drop back on the pillow. "Definitely. The good news is that you never have to be on your own at Christmas again."

Xander blinked. "Why does that sound almost like a threat?"

I laughed. "It is. You told me you loved me and now you have to keep me, Christmas decorations and all. Are you ready for that, Xander Cole?"

Xander leaned up on my chest until he was looking directly into my face, a slow smile spreading across his face. "I'm *so* ready for that."

I craned my neck to kiss him, but he moved out of reach, a pensive expression on his face.

I trailed my fingers over the lines on his brow. "What?"

"Move in with me."

Whatever I'd expected him to say, it wasn't that. A crazy thrumming started up in my chest, but I pushed it down and forced myself to think rationally. "I'd probably drive you crazy."

Xander smirked. "Most definitely, but in a good way."

"We should probably give it more time. You know, maybe go on a second date before we make a commitment like that."

He shrugged. "Fine. We'll do that tomorrow. You can move in on Friday. We can squeeze a third date in on Thursday if it makes you feel better."

"I haven't even unpacked the boxes in my new place yet."

Xander poked me in the chest. "Great. All the easier to move, then."

Logic crumbled away, leaving nothing but emotion in its place. Emotion and want. There was nothing I wanted more, and to hell with whether it was too fast. It would either work or it wouldn't, and the second option just wasn't going to happen. I wouldn't let it.

Xander raised an eyebrow. "Say yes."

"Yes." It was the easiest word I'd ever said.

EPILOGUE

11 months later

Xander

It was easier to knock than to search through my pockets for the key. The door swung open almost immediately, the man lounging in the doorway giving me a slow once over, his eyes narrowing on the leather jacket I wore. He crossed his arms over his chest and regarded me coolly. "Are you a salesman or a carol singer?"

I cleared my throat and sang the first two lines of "We Three Kings of Orient Are," managing not to sing 'one in a taxi and one in a car' for the second line, which in itself deserved recognition for my amazing powers of restraint.

The man reared back in a way that said my rendition had caused him actual physical pain. "A salesman, then. What are you selling?"

I dropped my gaze to my suitcase before inspiration struck. I pulled at the collar of the jacket. "I've got this to sell."

He looked decidedly unimpressed. "You can't sell a *stolen* jacket back to its owner. Its owner who spent a whole day looking for it before working out that their thieving boyfriend must have taken it, even though he has several jackets of his own that are far more expensive and far more suited to the current weather."

I let out a huff. "You say stolen, I say borrowed."

He pulled out his phone. "We should let the police sort it out. They can also investigate how criminal your singing is while they're here. I reckon being that far away from the actual tune deserves a custodial sentence. He pressed a button on his phone. "That's the first nine that I've just pressed. I'm now going for the second one, which I will follow with the…"

I grinned at having my own words thrown back at me, and then I couldn't hold back any longer, throwing myself into his arms so energetically that Ferris staggered backwards under my weight. "God, I missed you."

He didn't get a chance to respond until I'd finished kissing him long and hard. Everything I might have needed him to say was already there in the hungry and desperate way he kissed me back. I rested my forehead against his, his fingers wrapping around the lapels of the jacket that I'd borrowed because it reminded me of him. Well, that and the fact I looked good in it. "How long have I been away?"

Ferris lifted his head to stare at me, love shining in his eyes. It was a look I never got tired of seeing. "It feels like a year, but I think it was a week. Welcome home."

I kissed him again for good measure before reluctantly disentangling myself from him to retrieve my suitcase from where I'd left it outside the door. The door that was open, allowing anyone who might have passed in the last five minutes front row seats to our passionate reunion.

It was only when I turned back that I caught sight of what had happened to my hallway in my absence, the whole thing covered from top to toe in twinkling fairy lights. They were everywhere—ceiling, banister, walls. "Jesus Christ!"

Ferris chuckled. "See! You're getting into the Christmas spirit already and remembering what it's all about." He flung out a hand like the best sort of quiz show host. "What do you think? I may have been slightly bored without you here."

"Bored. How? You've been working. And I thought you were picking up extra shifts?" I was still staring at the fairy lights. I knew how deer felt now when they were transfixed by headlights and couldn't look away.

"Look." Ferris rushed over to a small control panel. He proceeded to walk me though twelve thousand different ways in which they could flash. "Impressive, huh?"

"I'm not sure that's the word I'd use."

Ferris cocked his head to one side. "Are you upset that I started decorating without you? Don't be. We can do the outside lights together."

"Outside lights." I picked up my suitcase and dragged it down the hall. "Good! Because I was worried that people wouldn't be able to see the house from space. If you'd done them earlier, I could have got the pilot to head straight for here instead of Heathrow. I could have parachuted through the window."

Ferris walked over and slid his hands beneath my jacket, easing it off my shoulders. "Not a good idea. This Christmas, I want you with absolutely nothing broken."

I eyed him suspiciously. "Are you trying to undress me or take your jacket back?"

His grin said he'd been caught red-handed. "Both."

I took a moment to stand by the kitchen window and look out. Much to Ferris's disappointment, there hadn't been any snow this year. I intended to fix that after Christmas by springing a surprise holiday to Austria on him. Not skiing. Definitely not skiing. Hell would freeze over before I would ever set foot on a ski slope again. I just needed to organize Ferris having time off work without him getting wind of it so the surprise wouldn't be ruined.

I thought back over the past year. My life had changed in so many ways. Ferris had moved in almost straightaway, and we'd never looked back. That wasn't to say that everything had been plain sailing. It had taken time to fill in the cracks of me having to travel so much for work. Phone sex was never going to be an adequate substitute for long absences, but eventually we'd found our groove and we'd made it work. And it wasn't like my face was going to be in demand forever.

The slight hubbub of noise that had been in the background grew louder and then faded away again, telling me that someone had left the living room where the party was going on. Sure enough, footsteps sounded down the hall, and then arms wrapped around me from behind, Ferris's chin coming to rest on my shoulder. "I missed you."

"I've only been gone five minutes."

"I still missed you." I watched Ferris's reflection lift his head to stare in the same direction I was. "What are we looking at?"

I covered his hands with mine. "Nothing in particular."

"Ah, I see. You're practicing your modeling. I didn't realise looking mean and moody and staring off into the distance required practice. You don't need to. You've already got it down pat."

I inclined my head in the direction of the living room. "How is everyone? Are they okay?"

Ferris rubbed his chin on my shoulder. "Well… Mia is regaling my mum with torrid tales of wardrobe malfunctions at catwalk shows. I can't quite decide whether the look on my mum's face is fascination or horror. Probably a bit of both. Meanwhile, Robert is still being very sweet to her and waiting on her hand and foot. He's a hundred times better than Barry ever was, and I fully approve. Miles is telling everyone who cares to listen that he should be in Spain with the kids and that going there for New Year instead doesn't feel right. My friend, Emma, is getting steadily drunker and increasingly touchy feely with your model friend with the complicated Mexican name that I can never remember. The poor man looks scared out of his mind. Oh, and Doctor Murphy is talking to anyone who's polite enough to listen, which is really only Dorothy. She may have found the one man who won't be put off by Brandon being straight and married."

I laughed. "Remind me why you invited Chris Murphy again? I did tell you he once tried to chat me up and called you annoying, right?"

Ferris snorted. "I didn't invite him. This is what he does. He just turns up at places. *You* let him in."

I turned in his arms to face him. "Only because I thought you'd invited him."

Ferris shrugged, his lips twitching. "But seriously, are you okay? We can throw them all out if you want."

I shook my head. "I just wanted a breather. And then I started thinking about the last year, about how much better my life is with you in it, and what a weird series of events had to fall into place for that to happen—skiing, the accident, Miles not being able to find a nurse, your flat flooding, Barry being there so you couldn't stay with your mum."

Ferris dipped his head to brush his lips over mine. "I like to think it was fate. I also like to think that if we hadn't met that way, we would have bumped into each other some way."

I thought about it. "If you'd met me in a bar, what would you have done?"

Ferris's grin was nothing short of wicked. "I would have pulled out all my best chat up lines. And you would have rolled your eyes at me and pretended you weren't interested."

I smiled. I could almost picture it, and he was right. That's exactly how it would have happened. "And then we would have ended up in bed together anyway."

Ferris nodded. "Definitely. It might have taken a bit longer to get there, but we would have ended up at exactly the same point. There's no getting rid of me."

I stared into the eyes of the man I loved, the man I would do anything for. "A Ferris is for life, not just for Christmas."

Ferris winked. "Exactly."

The End

·♥·♥·♥·♥·♥·

Want to read a bonus Ferris and Xander story? Sign up here – the download link is in the welcome email when you sign up. If you don't get it, check your spam folder.

THANKS

Thanks for reading this book. If you can take the time to leave a review, I would really appreciate it.

You can receive a number of FREE short stories and bonus chapters by signing up to my mailing list. You'll also be informed about new releases and get other exclusive stuff.

Want to see what I am working on before anyone else? Subscribe to my Patreon for WIP chapters and a version of A Temporary Situation written from Tristan's point of view. I'll also be writing bonus stories about established characters exclusive to my patrons.

Other places you can find me
Twitter. Bookbub Instagram Facebook. Website Days Den

MORE MM ROMANCE BOOKS BY H.L DAY

Romantic comedies
A Temporary Situation
A Christmas Situation
Temporary Insanity
Taking Love's Lead

Suspense
A Dance too Far
A Step too Far

Contemporary
Eager For You
Eager For More
Edge of Living
Kept in the Dark
Time for a Change
Christmas Riches

Post-apocalyptic Sci-fi
Refuge
Rebellion
Exposed

Paranormal
The Beauty Within

The Longest Night
Read the blurb for these books through H.L Day's <u>website</u> or on H.L Day's
<u>Amazon page</u>.

·♥·♥·♥·♥·♥·

<u>Available In audio</u>
Kept in the Dark
Edge of Living
A Dance too Far
A Step too Far
Exposed

IF YOU LIKED THIS BOOK YOU MAY ALSO LIKE

A Temporary Situation: An employee/boss gay romantic comedy
(Temporary; Tristan and Dom #1)

Personal assistant Dominic is a consummate professional. Funny then, that he harbors such unprofessional feelings toward Tristan Maxwell, the CEO of the company. No, not in that way. The man may be the walking epitome of gorgeousness dressed up in a designer suit. But, Dominic's immune. Unlike most of the workforce, he can see through the pretty facade to the arrogant, self-entitled asshole below. It's lucky then, that the man's easy enough to avoid.

Disaster strikes when Dominic finds himself having to work in close proximity as Tristan's P.A. The man is infuriatingly unflappable, infuriatingly good-humored, and infuriatingly unorthodox. In short, just infuriating. A late-night rescue leading to a drunken pass only complicates matters further, especially with the discovery that Tristan is both straight and engaged.

Hatred turns to tolerance, tolerance to friendship, and friendship to mutual passion. One thing's for sure, if Tristan sets his sights on Dominic, there's no way Dominic has the necessary armor or willpower to keep a force of nature like Tristan at bay for long, no matter how unprofessional a relationship with the boss might be. He may just have to revise everything he previously thought and believed in for a chance at love.

Buy now from Amazon

·♥·♥·♥·♥·♥·

Temporary Insanity: An enemies to lover gay romantic comedy. (Temporary; Paul and Indy #1)

Sleeping with the enemy never felt so good.

When Paul Davenport comes face to face with the man he caught in bed with his boyfriend years before, it's hate at first sight. Well, second sight. Indy should be apologizing, not flirting. Except the gorgeous barman is completely oblivious to their paths ever having crossed before.

Despite his feelings, Paul's powerless to resist the full-on charm offensive that follows. It's fine though. It's just sex. No emotions. No getting to know each other. Just a bout of temporary insanity that's sure to run its course once the simmering passion starts to wear off.

Only what if it's not? Indy's nothing like the man Paul expected him to be from his past actions. What if they're perfect for each other and Paul's just too stubborn to see it? Forging a relationship with him would require an emotional U-turn Paul might not be capable of making.

There's a thin line between love and hate, and Paul's about to discover just how thin it really is. He can't possibly be falling for the man that ruined his life. Can he?

Warning: This book contains hate sex—sort of, lots of banter, and a pink elephant. No, really it does. Actually, two elephants.
Please note: Although this book is in the Temporary series, it occurs during the same timeline as A Temporary Situation. Therefore, both books can be read as standalones and in any order.

Buy from Amazon

·❤·❤·❤·❤·❤·

Time for a Change: A Grumpy vs Sunshine gay romance
What if the last thing you want, might be the very thing you need?

Stuffy and uptight accountant Michael's life is exactly the way he likes it: ordered, routine and risk-free. He doesn't need chaos and he doesn't need anything shaking it up and causing him anxiety. The only blot on the horizon is the small matter of getting his ex-boyfriend Christian back. That's exactly the type of man Michael goes for: cultured, suave and sophisticated.

Coffee shop employee Sam is none of those things. He's a ball of energy and happiness who thinks nothing of flaunting his half-naked muscular body and devastating smile in front of Michael when he's trying to work. He knows what he wants—and that's Michael. And no matter how much Michael tries to resist him, he's not going to take no for an answer.

Sam eventually chips through Michael's barriers and straight into his bed. But Michael's already made some questionable decisions that might just come back to haunt him. He's got some difficult choices to make if he's ever going to find love. And he might just find that he's too set in his ways to make the right ones quickly enough. If Michael's not careful, the best thing that's ever happened to him might just slip right through his fingers. Because even a patient man like Sam has his limits.

Buy from Amazon

·♥·♥·♥·♥·♥·

Taking Love's Lead: An opposites attract gay romance
Sometimes you've got to stalk a man to win his heart.

A whirlwind encounter has web designer Zachary Cole reassessing his life and what he wants from it. Knocked for six by a less than orthodox meeting with the sexy Edgar, he resolves to see him again. Even if it does involve hatching a plan using his heavily pregnant sister, her dalmatian, and a rather large dose of subterfuge.

Sick of being dumped, dog-walker Edgar's sworn off relationships. Zack might just happen to pop up wherever he goes, but that's not going to change anything. It's not like Zack would ever want anything more than a walk on the wild side with him anyway. They're just too different. He'll stick to his four-legged friends instead. They might get up to a lot of mischief but they never let him down.

Zack wants love. Edgar only wants friendship. Can the two men find common ground amid the chaos of Edgar's life? Or is Zack going to find that no matter what he does, he'll end up having to walk away?

A romantic comedy full of mad mishaps with dogs, ducks, and lakes. Oh, and two stubborn men as well who find it almost impossible to both be on the same

page.
Buy from Amazon

Printed in Great Britain
by Amazon